The Dark Of October

B. D. West

Bdwestpublishing

Cover design by: ebooklaunch.com

Published by: bdwestpublishing

ISBN source: 978-1-7370178-2-0

Author B. D. West

P.O. Box 2034

Bryson City, NC 28713

2021

authorbdwest.com

More From B. D. West

The Wynter Timber Saga

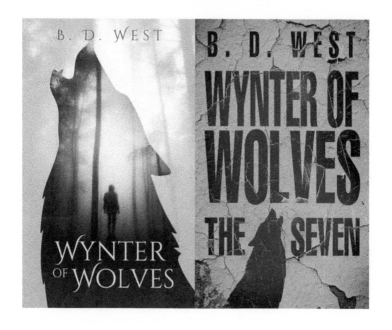

Available where most books are sold

Dedication

I would like to dedicate this book to my fans. Without you, none of this would be possible. It has been an incredible journey to discover so many kindred spirits. You are my people and the reason I continue writing every day. I dedicate this book to my husband, Eric. You make writing fun and an adventure. You make sense of it all and I thank you for that. Thank you to my biggest fans, my son Dakota and my mom. Thank you for your excitement about my books and for your humor as I chase my dreams. Thank you, mom for dressing up as a witch every year without fail, for reminding me to never stop being an overgrown child at heart, making candy bars a food group for one night and for making Halloween special for me.

I dedicate this short story collection to the people who love October and the chilly fall months.

THE DARK OF OCTOBER

A SHORT STORY COLLECTION

B. D. WEST

Table of Contents

The enchanting month of October burns forever in my mind. The crisp fall air, the earthy smells from the leaves on the ground, warm sweaters, children running around in costumes in search of free candy and the burning wood crackling in the firepit outside. October reminds me to wake up my inner child from her adult life. I get excited to hear spooky stories being told by my fellow fall lovers. Apples, pumpkin spice and cinnamon fill the air in every store I visit. October is a magical time for children and for grownups. Wake up your inner child and enter my world in the dark of October.

~B. D. West

The Long Ride Home

Randy looked at the entrance to the Coleman coalmine through the dusty windshield of his 1975 truck. Every bone in his body throbbed from the twelve-hour shift he just pulled. Wiping the perspiration from his brow, he cursed under his breath as he glanced down at his wet, blackened hand. Randy was sick of the coal dust. It weighed heavily on his lungs and ruined every piece of clothing he owned. The Coleman coalmine was the only job that paid worth a damn in West Virginia, and he had people relying on him to keep them fed. Every day he felt the coalmine taking a little piece of his soul. He had worked underground since he was a young man. Randy couldn't remember that person anymore. The only person left was a tired old man with no dreams left to dream. Sleep, work, go home, eat supper, rinse and repeat. That was his life now. Shaking his weary head, he rolled his window down and started up the engine. That old familiar roar comforted him like a mother soothing her baby to sleep.

As Randy pulled out onto the street, he thought of his father. He had bought the truck brand new when Randy was five years old. His dad used to go around telling everybody how it was a heavy duty, half-ton pickup truck. His father was so proud of his truck. Randy remembered the day he brought it home. His father took the entire family for a ride. He told Randy's mother that he had it all, the American dream. Randy smirked at the very idea of the American dream today. Today the American dream is to generate as much money as you can. Both parents work and leave the kids at home. Kids today are called latchkey kids. In Randy's day, the kids could walk home from school without too much worry. The moms were at home with milk and cookies on the table. Well, at least that was Randy's mom's routine. His mom would look astonished when she would find out a single woman moved into the neighborhood. It was unheard of for a woman to work to support her children.

Randy's mother never had a job in her life until his father died ten years after he bought that truck. His mother took care of it for him since he was the only boy. He had three sisters, and not one of them showed interest in the truck. Now it was Randy's turn to drive his father's truck and feel proud of his American dream.

The American dream feeling never touched him like it did for his father. All he could feel was depression. The American dream didn't quite work out for him. He and his wife tried like hell to have a baby. When they went to the Doctor to find out why they couldn't conceive, they found out she had ovarian cancer. She had a hysterectomy by the age of twenty-five.

To top off his American dream, his wife's parents came to live at their house. The home he purchased was modest. The living conditions were cramped. Her parents were feeble and required all of Sandy's care. She barely had any time for Randy. If she wasn't running errands for her parents, she was sleeping or doing something related to their care. She did it all, except for investing time with him.

Randy's reflections cut short when his headlights caught a man in the distance. He squinted his eyes and worked to make out who it was. The stranger was bent over, tying his shoe. As Randy got closer to the man, he recognized Gene, his childhood friend. Randy pulled over and honked his horn. Gene came running. He peered through the glass with a gigantic grin on his face before opening the door and climbing in.

"Well... if it ain't Gene, Gene the love machine!" Randy said in his best teasing voice.

"If it ain't dandy, Randy!" Gene replied.

"Well, I don't know if looking dandy is the word I would use for how I look right now, man." Randy said as he struggled in vain to dust off his pants. "Where have you been, man? Geez! When is the last time we hung out?" Randy pulled out onto the street as Gene chuckled.

"I couldn't tell you, but we're here now. That should count for something." Gene said with a snicker.

Randy, struck with inspiration, looked over at Gene. "Are you heading anywhere?"

"Well... not yet, why?"

Randy grinned as he shot down a familiar back road. He could drive this dirt road with a blindfold on. It was a route he had spent many hours as a teenager camping, fishing and making out with girls. He brought his truck to a stop in front of Township Lake. The headlights cast an eerie glow on the silent black water in front of them. Randy remembered how all the kids used to call it Shipwreck Cove. Randy figured it was because of the boating accidents that took place there and the Jet Ski's resting at the bottom of the lake. He recalled all the years Gene had talked him into playing hooky at Shipwreck Cove just to inhale a few beers. Shipwreck Cove was a tradition back in Randy's youth. Everyone who was anyone went there.

"Man, if this place could talk." Gene said as he rolled down the window and hung his elbow out.

"You sure talked me into some crazy shenanigans."

"As I recall, it was you who brought that Jack Daniels bottle and dared me to drain half of it without taking a breath. You know, I went home and felt like the puke fest would never end. My mom thought I had the flu! She took me to the doctor and everything."

"Oh man, you never told me that!" Gene erupted into fits of laughter. "Do you remember how you told me I could catch a fish if I swam naked?" Gene lowered his voice to sound like Randy. "Just use nature's bait and tackle, Gene."

"Yeah, and you tried it too!" Randy said as he chuckled.

"Yeah, well, when something bumped into me, I thought for sure I was going to die. I was sick for a week after swimming in that frigid water." Gene added, as he laughed harder.

Randy climbed out of the truck and reached into a cooler in the truck's bed. He plucked out a beer and popped it open. "You want one?" He asked as he held up the can of beer in the air.

"No, thanks." Gene said as he climbed out of the truck.

"Well, suit yourself." Randy said before he took a huge gulp. He strolled over to the lake's edge and watched the water wash up against the muddy bank, and then, as it retreated into the darkness. A twinge of depression washed over him. "Why do those good times disappear, man?" Randy whispered.

"What do you mean? There are still good times to be had. It could be worse. You could be dead." Gene said with a smile.

"Well, there's that I guess." Randy replied with an exhausted grin. "I mean, I had plans for my life and now it's just gone."

"I think you had your father's plan for your life. You tried to live up to what he was. Live your life the way your life is meant to be. If you can't be happy where you are, you'll never be content anywhere you go. Life is short; too short, if you ask me. Don't waste it on being miserable." Gene placed his hand on the back of Randy's shoulder. "If you think long and hard about your life, you might just see the good qualities that you missed. Trust me when I tell you, you are not stuck. Anyone can change their life. You just need to find the courage to do it."

Randy wiped a tear off his grimy cheeks and smirked. "Gene, Gene, the advice machine?"

Gene chuckled. "Maybe so, my friend... maybe so."

Randy took in the last drink of his beer and wandered over to his truck. He threw the empty can back into the cooler. Seeing all he needed to see of the past, Randy climbed into the truck. Gene walked over to the passenger side and clambered in. They rode in silence until Randy pulled out onto the main road once again. Randy felt like he was in a trance as he considered his dead-end job, the wife that neglected him and how disappointed his father would be at how his life turned out.

Gene interrupted the thick silence as he spoke up. "You can let me out right there."

Randy shook his head in confusion. "Fox Hill cemetery? I can't leave you there. It's not safe. Come on, let me take you home." Gene shook his head, no. Reluctantly, Randy pulled off the road in front of the Fox Hill cemetery's entrance. He couldn't think of a suitable reason to keep Gene in his truck. He watched with a heavy heart as Gene exited the vehicle.

Gene closed the door and turned around. He leaned in through the window with a grin. "Randy, I'm fine. I'm more at home in that cemetery than I am anywhere else. Besides, I like it there. Trust me, it's ok. Go home to your family and remember what I said." Gene gave one last smile before he swung around and strolled up the hillside.

Randy stared in disbelief as he watched Gene disappear into the wooded cemetery. He cranked his truck back to life and headed home like Gene told him to. His tiny home was full of life as he pulled into the driveway. All the windows were lit, and smoke poured from the chimney. It felt welcoming.

After climbing out of the truck, Randy strolled into the house. He made his way into the kitchen, where Sandy was washing up the supper dishes. He sat down in one of the kitchen chairs.

Sandy's long black hair swung over her shoulder and across her back as she glanced at him. She grinned that schoolgirl smile Randy had fallen for when they were teenagers. "You want some coffee? I just made a fresh pot."

"Yeah, that would be great." Randy said as he leaned down to take off his work boots. "You'll never guess who I ran into on the way home." Randy said as he fought with a knot that had formed in his shoelaces. He could hear Sandy walking around, preparing a cup of coffee for him.

"Babe, I have no energy to guess tonight. It's been a long day. Who did you see?" she answered as she poured the coffee.

"It was my old buddy, Gene. Gosh, he looked great. I have not seen him in well… I don't know how long. I tell you; I was feeling low tonight thinking about my old man and my crappy job." Randy said as he kicked off the first boot and went to work on the next set of knots in the other boot. "There was Gene on the side of the road. I pulled over and he climbed in my truck. Before I knew it, we were down at Shipwreck Cove having a beer. Well, I was enjoying a beer. We talked about old times and all the ridiculous things we did as a kid. I felt like an ass, but I told him about how depressed I was. He made me feel so much better. You know, we should invite him over for dinner or something. Maybe he could bring his wife. Remember Sherri? You could make one of your famous apple pies." Randy sat up and kicked off the last boot. He looked up at Sandy and was startled by her expression. She was standing like a statue with her big blue eyes wide with fright. She held Randy's cup of coffee in midair as if she were fixing to hand the cup over to him.

Randy jumped up and ran to her. "Sandy, what is it? What's the matter?" Sandy blinked a few times and searched Randy's face for any sign that he may be joking with her.

"Randy, that's not funny." Sandy spoke in a whispered tone.

"What? What's not funny?" Randy replied, bewildered.

"Randy, don't you remember? Gene died three years ago?" Sandy stared at Randy with a mixture of pity and fear. "He died in an automobile accident. Don't you remember?"

Randy stumbled over to his chair and sat down. His blood felt like it was rushing out of his body as the memories of the news of Gene's death filled his mind. He recalled all too well the heartache he felt at Gene's burial at Fox Hill cemetery. Randy laughed to himself in shock as the thought rolled through his mind; "I guess Gene was right. Things could be worse. I could be dead..."

Haint Susie

The year was nineteen forty-one. I was ten years old. It was the year everyone started calling me little Sue. To be honest, I despised it. But I adored the woman I was named after. My Aunt Susie was my favorite person in the entire world besides my mom. I spent every summer at her house in the Dry Creek holler. Everyone who lived in Dry Creek was poor, but I don't think they noticed it. Living off the bounty of the farmland was a guarantee you had food in your stomach and a roof over your head at night. I had no clue that kind of existence was poor to the rest of the world.

I know you haven't heard of this place. Most people haven't. It was one of the poorest places to live in Tennessee. If you grew up there, you would never forget it. It was a place where wildflowers grew. You could pass acre after acre of farmland and never tire of staring at the limitless fields. You drove through creek beds to reach your driveway, and elderly folks waved from their front porch as you rode by.

My mother worked for a factory sewing dresses for department stores. When the war started, the military took the workshop over. She sewed clothing for our boys who were fighting in the war. My father died in the first few weeks of World War two. My mom regarded it as her duty to this country and to honor her husband by sewing uniforms for the soldiers. I would go to my Aunt Susie's farm every summer. School would be out for the summer, and my mother couldn't afford a babysitter. My Aunt Susie always said watching us youngsters was her doing her part for the war effort. I think she didn't want to be alone. She wasn't alone with me and my three brothers running around.

Aunt Susie's husband had drowned in a flash flood while my mom was pregnant with me. She refused to re-marry. Her farm was her great passion after her husband's death. She threw herself into the vegetable garden, chicken coupes and flowerbeds. She worked me to death all sum-mer long in the sweltering heat. I wouldn't have traded it for nothing. She suffered a stroke in nineteen thirty-eight. Don't think that slowed her down one bit. Aunt Susie could speak and use her hands, but she never regained the use of her left leg. She told us kids she had turned into a pirate and someday she just might get a peg leg. She snorted with delight as she took a step with her good leg and drug her left foot behind her as she chased us around.

When I learned my aunt had passed, it took me a few hours to process what that meant. I understood what death was, but I never went to funerals. My mother would leave me with friends if someone died. She said I was too young, or I didn't need to witness something like that. This time, when she tried to leave me and my brothers with an ac-quaintance, I refused. I don't know why. Something inside me had to see her one more time.

The more my mother protested, the louder I became. I pointed out to her I was three years away from becoming a teenager and that I was practically a woman. My mother either listened to reason or she became exhausted from ar-guing with me. I didn't care either way as long as I got to go. I didn't know what I was asking for.

In the holler, no one could afford a lavish funeral. If someone passed, you had the wake and then the burial the next day. You had to do it fast. It was too expensive to have someone in a funeral home for three days and then buried. Nope, in Dry Creek, you got a wooden casket and a wake.

I didn't know what a wake was until I arrived at Aunt Susie's home. More people were there than I expected. Some people walked, and some rode horses.

There were a few people that could afford an automobile to drive. My mother's employer was kind enough to let her borrow his truck. It was a nineteen twenty-four model pickup truck. It was loud, but it worked. I didn't know her boss had been teaching her to drive on her lunch breaks. He dropped it off at our house the night before we left. I didn't like the way he grinned at her or the way she smiled at him. I didn't ask her about him because it made me angry. I had other matters to think about.

Mom parked the truck between the creek bed and Aunt Susie's flower garden. I don't know why, but it made me furious to look at all those people wandering around Aunt Susie's farm. After all, I had helped her plant those rows of squash and butter beans. I had helped Aunt Susie pick out the seeds to every single flower around the farm. Who were these people tramping all over our hard work?

My mom grabbed a suitcase she had packed for her and me to share. Next, she took my hand and led me into Aunt Susie's cabin. Aunt Susie's cabin was packed wall to wall with people dressed in black. Some were singing Amazing Grace, and others were sniffing back tears. I was too short to see Aunt Susie as my mother pulled me to the back room. She brought us into Aunt Susie's room and placed our suitcase on the bed. Turning to me, she tried to smile as she dusted off my dress. "Are you positive you want to see her, little Sue?"

I shook my head and my face felt numb as I responded. "Yes."

My mother looked me over one last time. "Alright."

She took me by the hand and led me out of Aunt Susie's room and through the crowd. My heart hammered in my rib cage as I approached the wooden casket resting on Aunt Susie's kitchen table. I peered into the casket, and it surprised me to see that she looked asleep. Someone had dressed her in her night gown and crossed her hands over her stomach. I glanced up at my mother and silent tears were streaming down her face. She grasped my hand tight as she wept.

We sat through at least three hours of singing and two preachers taking turns telling everyone to pray and repent. I suppose the preachers saw the funeral as an excellent occasion to save a few souls. I heard little of it. My sadness drowned out most of their speeches.

By noon, we were on a hillside looking down in a six-foot hole. Aunt Susie's wooden casket had been nailed shut and lowered into the ground. The sun above me burned my scalp, and my dress was roasting me like a Thanksgiving turkey. I preferred to wear my overalls, but my mother insisted I put on the white dress with the faded pink flowers she had made me for Easter. At least she didn't make me wear shoes. Mom was so proud of the dress she had sewn from the material she purchased for a penny at Owen's Feed and Seed. It was the same cloth they used to put flour in. She had been saving a small roll of lace she found in the factory garbage for such an occasion. The lace scratched my neck. I never wore lace again.

I remained by Aunt Susie's grave until every mourner had gone home. My mother waited for me until the sun set. She placed her arm around me. "Little Sue, we have to go; it's getting dark." She took me by the hand and led me down the dirt road back to Aunt Susie's house.

All the automobiles, people, and horses were gone. It was just me and my mom standing in front of Aunt Susie's cabin. It made me sick to look at the muddy tire marks left behind in the damaged grass.

My feet were caked with road dust and mud. My mother pumped some water into a bucket and carried it over to the porch. She asked me to sit down on the front steps so she could wash my feet. I dreaded to go back into the cabin. I didn't want to sleep there, but mom said she had not learned to drive at night. After she scrubbed my feet, we went into the darkened house. Aunt Susie never saw the point of electricity, and she never had it installed. We had to make do with the oil lamps she had placed around the house. While mom attempted to reheat some cornbread and beans on the wood stove, I stood in the middle of the living room.

I glanced around and my heart fell. No one bothered to place the table back in the kitchen, and Aunt Susie's wooden chairs were strewn all over the house. The room stunk of warm silk flowers and a variety of perfumes the ladies that attended had worn. It made me sick to my stomach. I shifted away from the heartbreaking sight and headed for Aunt Susie's bedroom. It still smelled like her. Her bathrobe was folded over the back of her vanity chair.

Her hairbrush still had her grey hair sticking out of it. My eyes burned as I spotted her lotion bottle sitting on the edge of her vanity. It looked like she had just put some on. The cherry blossom scent wafted from the bottle into the air. At that moment, I could have sworn she was in the room.

I yanked off my dress and kicked it into the corner of the room. My watery eyes glared back at me from the vanity mirror as I stood in my white silk slip. The anguish on my face was too much for me to carry.

I twisted away from the mirror and ambled over to Aunt Susie's bed. It was still made. Aunt Susie had consistently made her bed every day without fail. She said it kept her sane. I never knew what she meant by that, but it always made me giggle.

Pulling back the heavy blankets, I passed my hand against the crisp sheets underneath. Aunt Susie kept her sheets so soft. I slipped underneath the covers. I fell asleep immediately.

That same night, I awoke with a jerk. I'm not certain what woke me, but I was wide awake. I glanced beside me, and my mother was sound asleep. A cool breeze blew in from the windows my mother had left open. The open windows let in an eerie blue light the moon cast into the room. I drew the blankets against my collar to shelter myself from the summer night chill.

As I began to fall asleep, I heard it. I don't know if you will believe me or not, but I heard it. Stomp... drag. Stomp... drag. Stomp... drag. Stomp... drag.

The noise started in the kitchen; faint at first. Then, as the noise grew closer to the bedroom door, it became louder. STOMP... drag. STOMP... drag. STOMP... drag. STOMP... drag.

My body became crippled with fear. I couldn't move. I lay powerless on my back beside of my mother. I couldn't move a finger or a toe. My lips trembled as I struggled to form words to yell for help. Each time I tried, STOMP... drag. STOMP... drag. STOMP... drag. STOMP... drag.

I watched the doorway as terror shot through my veins. Something was coming down the corridor. It headed straight for my room. STOMP... drag. STOMP... drag. STOMP... drag. STOMP... drag. And suddenly it halted outside of the door. I stared in horror as a translucent figure of my aunt came through the door. I tried to scream, but my vocal cords were too dry.

Aunt Susie took steps to the end of my bed. Stomp... drag. Stomp... drag. Stomp... drag. Stop.

She angled her face in my direction. She then took her shadowy hands and arranged them on the blankets. I felt the bed move up and down as she checked the mattress to determine how comfortable it was. Next, she tilted her head and looked at me. She lifted her boney finger to her lips as if to tell me to be quiet. I couldn't nod my head, nor could I answer. She didn't wait for an answer.

Aunt Susie stood up straight and glanced over at her vanity. She pointed her finger at a pendant dangling from the mirror and then back to me. She repeated the gesture several times. I could only assume she wanted me to have her necklace as a gift. I finally plucked up the courage to shake my head to let her see I understood. I thought that would make her go away.

It didn't.

She seemed amused that I could see her, and I understood what she wanted. She paused in the middle of the room as if she were trying to memorize how her room looked.

Next, she turned her translucent gaze on me. My body became tense and cold. Why wouldn't she leave? What else could she possibly want from me?

Aunt Susie turned her body towards me and began her sickening walk once more. Stomp… drag. Stomp… drag. Stomp… drag. Stomp… drag. Stomp… drag.

Aunt Susie stood over me. As she peered down at me, I could smell her. She smelled like a crisp, dingy cellar and the plastic flowers that covered her grave. I sought to scream once more, only air left my mouth. My throat was too constricted to allow sound to pass. I watched, horrified, as she leaned down and held out her hands in front of her. Her chilly hands moved through my body and touched the bed beneath me. Once again, she tested the mattress to see if it was comfortable enough for her. When convinced, she stood up and swung around.

Terror would never be a strong enough word to express the fear I was going through. I watched as she sat down on the bed. Her frosty body sat through me. The sensation made my stomach turn upside down. A small squeak escaped from my parched lips as she settled down on the bed. Her head passed through my chest as she curled up on the bed that was once hers. The room was frostier than the first morning in January. For a moment, I could see the breath that left my body.

Aunt Susie's body disappeared before my eyes. I remained frozen in place with my clammy hands gripping the blankets. Tears tumbled down my cheeks as the realization of what happened sank in. I risked a peek around the room. I was alone. I glanced over to my mother, who was untouched by Aunt Susie.

I didn't sleep a wink that night.

The next morning, my mother gathered our things and a few keepsakes from Aunt Susie's house. I, of course, took the pendant that Aunt Susie pointed out to me. My mother paused and stared at me with a puzzled expression. "Is that the one item you are choosing to remember Susie with?"

I glanced down at the polished round cameo studded with glittering gems. I nodded my head as I arranged the golden chain around my neck. "Yes."

"Funny you should choose that one. She instructed me over and over how she wanted you to have that." My mother stood for a minute before she chuckled to herself. "I guess something connected you two in spirit."

My mother did not know how I knew about the necklace. I wasn't about to tell her. I mean… who would believe me?

Who would believe that I had a visit from Haint Susie?

The Dark of October

The crackle of the campfire filled the chilly October air. Smoke swirled all around me. Warmth from the fiery logs encircled my body like a fleece blanket, swaddling me like a baby. The light cast by the fire bounced off the darkness. It never could penetrate the pitch black of the night, however. The dark gave everyone a deceptive sense of security. It was like we had an invisible wall protecting us from whatever was out there. I knew differently.

Looking around the campfire at the expectant faces staring at me, I prepared myself to tell the story. It would be hard for the teens to believe me, and none of them wanted to be there. If it were not for the court making them, they wouldn't waste their time with me. Each one of them had a petty offence they committed. Now, it was up to me to help them see the error of their ways. I cleared my throat before I began. "There are things in the darkness that you forget are there. Maybe you think the tales your grandparents told you were to make you stay out of the woods. Maybe the stories were to keep you out of trouble." Each of the young teens squirmed under the tension. "Perhaps you think adults want to tell you what to do and they don't want you to have any fun."

"Well, it's true. I heard from a kid at school there is nothing out there. When he went into the woods; nothing happened. Our parents don't want us to leave home. That's why we are here. They think you can scare us straight. Now we're stuck in this camp listening to your stupid campfire tale." Stacie said, as she creased her eyebrows and criss-crossed her arms.

"Yeah!" the other teens said, one by one.

"Is that what you think, Stacie? What about you, Tommie? Makayla? Robert?" I glanced around and waited for them to respond. Each one took turns looking at the other. One by one, they continued their stare into the fire. Some wrapped themselves in their blankets. The others peered into the unrelenting black night. I began again. "I am the only one who dares to speak the name of this powerful being. No one knows where it came from. Some claim it was a battered wife who came back for vengeance. Others suggest it is a troubled spirit that was previously a mortal man and returned from the grave to murder his killers. Well, I maintain it doesn't matter, all we need to know is that it's real."

"What's its name, Mrs. Martin?" Makayla asked timid.

"They call it… the wood crier." I glanced around. The teens snickered as they passed loaded looks to each other. "It may not be the name you expected, but that is the name you hear before you perish. The legend started hundreds of generations ago. Many accounts exist of inexperienced people traveling into the woodlands and never coming out." The laughter died down as my words settled in.

Satisfied I had their attention, I went on. "The first legend was of the youthful pioneer newlyweds. They settled right here on this very spot that we have our campfire. Elijah and his beautiful new bride were in love. They moved to the new world, hoping to discover a fresh way of life without the strict control of the queen. They craved an existence without the severe rules of their parents. Elijah went into the woods to hunt for food while his young bride remained at home. After a week of no news from Elijah, his inexperienced bride searched for him; she never came out of the woods."

I picked up a stick from the ground and nudged at the fire as I continued. "Then, there was the myth of a widow named Victoria. Before she had been widowed, she had been blessed with ten fine children: four boys and six girls. Victoria's children possessed beauty other people could only dream of. Oddly enough, the widow was not so blessed. Time and delivering too many children wore down any beauty she once had. She had mousy brown hair that she tamed into a bun at the nape of her neck. Her body was plump, and her hands were wrinkled beyond her years. The only thing beautiful about her was her smile. When Victoria purchased the land, she determined she had earned a break from the suffering she had endured. She had dreams of splendor. Her dreams were occupied with visions of a dwelling with many rooms for her children and occasional guest."

Smiling to myself as I envisioned the scene, I continued. "Victoria entertained the notion that she could open a bed-and-breakfast for travelers. Those dreams slowly deteriorated. Her sons erected a cramped wooden house to survive the harsh winter. Victoria watched in horror as her sons would head into the woods and they came back with one brother missing. They told the tale of someone crying in the distant woods. They would hear tree branches snapping as if someone were pacing back and forth. Then the shrieking and wailing would begin. It would start in the distance, then it would grow closer and closer. Fear would close in all around them, and they would run. After losing their brothers, the sisters had to take their place out of desperation for food."

The fire began to die out. I stood up and seized a nearby branch and fed the flames. After I returned to my seat, I continued my tale. "Until one day, the widow found herself with one daughter left. The two of them went for weeks without food. They struggled to survive on birds and rabbits that wondered into the yard. When the rabbits stopped coming, they had no alternative but to wonder into the woods... helpless. Well, as you know, they never came out either. The list goes on and on." I peeked around at the fear on their faces as they mustered up the courage to ask questions. It was Tommie who spoke first.

"I don't understand. I mean, why do you live here? If it's so terrible, why don't you leave?"

"Well, that is an excellent question, Tommie. Look around... it's a marvelous piece of land nestled in the center of the Smoky Mountains."

I waved my hand around as if they could see in the dark. "It's the home of waterfalls, rich green trees and plentiful fish. Its serenity alone draws people here, away from their hectic lives. I had the opportunity to help young teens, such as yourself; simple as that." I smiled smoothly.

"How long have you lived here?" Makayla asked with wide, childlike eyes.

"If I told you how long, I would give away my age. You know what they say... never ask a lady how old she is." I grinned with a wink.

"Have you heard anything out in the woods?" Robert inquired.

"Well, I have heard some things." I replied, as I wondered how far to take the story.

"Like what?" Makayla asked as she soaked in every detail.

"Well, things like limbs snapping, and the howling of wolves in the distance. You know, wolves can sound like crying, even screaming."

"Don't you think they made these stories up? I mean... don't you think if these tales were true the disappearances would be reported; like in the news? I mean, things like that don't go unnoticed." Stacie said, as a matter of fact. She tossed her hair from her shoulders with the back of her hand in a snotty huff. "I mean, come on, guys. She is just telling us this crap to intimidate us. Think about it. We are here staying in her camp as a punishment. The Judge thought we could learn a lesson in the woods. She is just trying to give us nightmares."

"Stacie, you are constantly a skeptic. I mean... my mom used to tell me ghost stories all the time. She said if they raise the hair on the back of your neck, they are true. I don't know about you, but I have hair standing up on the back of my neck and chills running down my arms. There must be some truth to her stories. I can feel it, can't you?" Makayla asked as she glanced around the campfire.

"I feel it running through me." Robert replied as he stood up to stretch. "I mean, look around. These woods are as old as time itself. They were here since the world was created. Who is to say there isn't more out there? I don't want to pretend I know it all but, there is evil as well as there is good. I think there is something out there just waiting."

"Oh my gosh, Robert, you can't be serious. I thought you were the most levelheaded guy here." Stacie said, as she rolled her eyes. "Mrs. Martin, please tell everybody you're joking. No one will sleep tonight."

"Why Stacie; are you scared? I bet you are." Tommie said as he poked her in the ribs.

"I'm not scared. I just know all of you are buying into this fairytale she created just to scare us for entertainment. Which I don't think is appropriate. We are here to do our time for our crime. We are not here to get lied to!" Stacie stood up and faced me.

"Now, out with it! It's not true, is it... you made it up! Tell them!" Stacie said, as she flapped her hand at Makayla, Tommie, and Robert. "Tell them the truth!"

A quiet grin stretched across my face as I stood up and stretched my legs. I glanced at each teenager and gestured for them to sit down. They did as they were instructed; Stacie gave up and sat down as well. "Now, aren't we all comfy? You're right, Stacie. I didn't tell you the whole truth. There is more to the story that I keep to myself, and for a good reason. However, I won't call myself a liar to accommodate you. I know the truth about the wood crier. It is an actual entity that exists." I stepped over to the darkness and peered into the woods. I looked up into the sky in deep reflection.

"Tell us, Mrs. Martin, you can trust us." Makayla said.

"I don't know that I should. The fear may take you in the end."

"She's doing it again, guys! Come on! I for one don't want to listen to this B.S." Stacie said, as she stood up.

"Shut up, Stacie. You're the one who got us into trouble. At least we don't have to sit in a cell in juvenile hall. We get to be here in God's country to relax instead. We all wanted to go to the beach, but no, you had to steal that sweater at the mall! Your daddy worked out this arrangement. It could have been worse. I, for one, am enjoying this. Stop being so controlling!" Robert replied as he gestured for Stacie to sit down.

"Come on, you two, stop with the lovers' spat so we can hear the rest of the story. We're sorry, Mrs. Martin, please go on. Those two fight all the time. We want to hear the rest, sincerely." Tommie looked around, and each one took turns shaking their head in agreement. Stacie nodded her head as she sat down in her seat.

I pulled myself away from the heavens and I rounded to look at them. "There is another story to include in the legend of the wood crier. It is suggested that the wood crier was the Goddess Achlys; she was the Goddess of eternal night, misery and sadness. She was magnificent, but her absolute beauty was never seen for what it was. She was cursed to always be in the dark. Only those who waited for the first light of the sun could catch a glimpse of her before she disappeared."

I tucked my hair behind my ear as I proceeded. "She fell in love with a mortal man; his name was Lukas. He was a colonist that had come to the new world with his family as a baby. Achlys knew no bounds, not in the way the humans did. She roamed from one continent to the other in the blink of an eye. One day, she found herself on the edge of these woods as the sun came up. Lukas came out onto the doorstep of his parent's cabin, and it happened. Lukas saw Achlys staring at him. The romance began."

I pointed to the edge of the woods. "Achlys stood every morning on the edge of the woods waiting for Lukas; right over there. Every day, Lukas was standing in front of his cabin, expecting to see her. This continued for months until Achlys could stand it no longer. She broke the rules and spoke to Lukas."

Makayla raised her hand to her heart. "And then what happened?"

"Achlys waited patiently for the dawn. Her heart felt light as air as she saw Lukas step outside to wait for her. Achlys held out her hands to Lukas. He ran to her and fell into her embrace. They made love like soulmates that were united forever. Achlys lost track of the time and her father found out. He stripped away her beauty; she became covered with boils, scabs and lacerations. They oozed pus and blood; they would never heal. Achlys feared what her lover would think of her new appearance, but she had to try. Achlys waited in her usual spot for Lukas. Her heart soared when she saw him coming out the front door. As the sun rose, however, Achlys appearance fell onto the eyes of her handsome lover."

This was the part that was painful for me to tell. A warm tear threatened to spill down my cheek. "Lukas froze on the edge of the woods, gawking at his once beautiful lover. He wanted to scream. He couldn't do anything but shake his head and mumble over and over, no. Grief stricken, Achlys' spirit caved in on itself. It filled her with fury. She swore to never allow young beauty to grace her with their presence."

"What happened to Lukas?" Tommie asked.

"She killed him, of course." I answered as I smirked. The sun started to rise behind the teens. I wiped away my tear as I watched the puzzled expressions staring back at me. Horror filled their faces as my nails grew five inches longer. My skin cracked and peeled open as it drained with pus filled boils and dripping blood. My hair dropped out in knotted clumps. "Why the long faces? Don't you know genuine beauty when you see it?" I laughed even though I felt nothing. "You with your doubt, Stacie... am I real now, sweetheart? All of you have such beautiful faces, full of hope for the future. What do I have? Eternal darkness, that's what! I get cursed for what? For love? He didn't love me back." I opened my mouth and let out an earsplitting wail. "I am the wood crier!"

Stacie screamed at the top of her lungs as the rest of the panic-stricken teens scrambled to their feet.

"You can't escape... I'm ravenous." I lunged for my prey; I never missed. They put up a delicious fight.

After the ripping and severing of flesh, I peered down at my blood-soaked body. I inspected my bloated abdomen, full of beauty. "They were pretty, but not as beautiful as me," I thought to myself as I licked my fingers clean.

I chuckled as I pondered how simple it was to hack into Stacie's father's computer. It was like shooting fish in a barrel.

I smoothed out what was left of my blood-soaked lump of hair on top of my head and headed back into the woods where my eternal night continues.

I am waiting in the darkness, whether you believe in me... or not.

Midnight Ride

Noah woke with a start. His sofa felt hot against his skin. Stale beer clung to his tongue as he raised his heavy head. Looking around his living room, Noah could see he had slept all day. The streetlamp shining through the window informed him his bender knocked him out cold. As he thought about yelling for his brother, Dakota, a realization hit him. He had left Dakota at Oliver's house party. Noah had promised he would be right back. Jumping up from the sofa, Noah took his keys off the coffee table. He glanced at his wristwatch. "Oh my gosh, it's three in the morning. He is going to kill me." Noah said as he flung open the front door.

Startled, Noah jumped at the sight of Dakota sitting like a statue on the porch. He stared into the darkness as if he could see something Noah couldn't. A creepy feeling passed over Noah as he shoved his keys into his pocket. "I was just on my way to pick you up, baby brother." Dakota didn't move. "Hey, are you ok?"

Dakota offered a slight nod of the head. His voice came out in a whisper. "I'm good, man."

Noah looked around. "How did you make it home?"

Unblinking, Dakota replied. "I walked and then..." He shook his head and went silent.

Noah's eyes bulged. "You did what? Oliver's house is just over the Georgia border! You are telling me you walked here to the Cherokee reservation from Georgia?"

Dakota shook his head. "Yeah... I mean, no."

Confused, Noah sat beside Dakota on the porch step. He reached into his pocket and drew out a pack of cigarettes. He plucked out a smoke and placed it between his lips. Noah gave Dakota a sideways glance as he lit the tip end of his cigarette. "So, either you walked here, or you didn't. Which one is it? How did you get home?"

A crease appeared on Dakota's brow as he explained. "Well, when you didn't come for me, I started walking. I tried to call you like, twenty times. It was dark, so I used my flashlight on my phone and started walking. I figured you would see me walking and pick me up. But..."

Guilt surged through Noah's body. "I'm sorry, man. I guess I got too drunk. I'm not sure how I made it home in one piece." Noah glanced at his pickup under the streetlamp and smirked. "I guess my old war pony lived to see another day."

Stone faced; Dakota nodded his head. "Yeah, I guess so."

"So, you walked the whole way?"

Dakota shook his head. "A car pulled over. I assumed it was you, but it wasn't."

"Really? Who was it?" Noah asked, puzzled.

"It was a woman."

Noah grinned. "Well, that would explain the stunned expression on your face."

Ignoring Noah's observation, Dakota continued. "I was walking along the highway. My legs were growing tired. I had been hiking for almost two hours. I was about to call you again when I heard a car pull up behind me. I was reluctant to look at first. I have heard of the perverts that patrol the highways for their next victim. Next thing you hear is, they get raped, murdered, and later the body is disposed of on a mountain trail."

"Yeah, like that one chick they found last year. A bear almost finished her off when a group of hunters found her."

Dakota nodded his head. "I glanced back, and it surprised me to discover a flashy red sports car. A dome light turned on and it illuminated the most magnificent creature I have ever seen."

Noah's grin returned. "What did she look like?"

"Well, I wandered around to the passenger side and opened the door. I leaned down to peek inside. This woman had chocolate colored hair and sharp blue eyes. She grinned at me and asked me if I was lost. I answered no. I informed her I was on my way back to the reservation. She smiled and patted the passenger seat and told me to climb in. I checked the back seat to make certain she wasn't helping a pervert boyfriend. There was no one there, so I got in."

"You realize that was stupid, right? I mean, she could have been one of those psycho killers. We have a bunch of those running around here since they built the casino."

Dakota shook his head. "No, she wasn't one of those women. I can't explain it. There I was, next to this gorgeous woman. I usually get nervous around women that pretty, but I felt relaxed. Before I realized what was going on, I was spilling my guts about my entire life. I told her about you, how our parents died, and you raised me. I mean, if I had known any government secrets, I would have told her everything I knew."

Noah snorted. "Well, you say she was a knockout. A pretty woman has a way of melting your brain."

"It was more than that. She had this hypnotic club music playing on her radio and she drove so fast I felt like I was drunk."

"If she was speeding, why didn't you get home earlier? You've been gone since last night."

"That's the strange part. She would stop at random places."

Noah felt confused. "Where did she stop?"

Dakota stared at the stars as he struggled to recall every detail. "She stopped at convenience stores, twenty-four-hour shopping centers and random houses."

"Did you go in with her?"

Dakota shook his head. "No, I stayed in her car. She would say, this will only take a second and she would leave me in the car. I didn't care. I wanted the moment to last."

Noah nodded his head. "Who wouldn't?"

"When she came out of the shopping center, she asked if I wanted to drive. I said hell yeah. I mean, who would pass up the chance to drive a sports car?"

"For real, man." Noah flicked his cigarette into the grass. "So where did you go?"

Dakota grinned. "I headed for the interstate. She didn't care. She just turned up the music and rolled down the windows. I felt this..." Pointing to his chest, he continued on. "I felt this rush of electricity all over me. I felt powerful, fast, and unbreakable. I pushed that car to ninety miles an hour. The other cars looked like a blur. I knew I could wreck, but it was like I was on drugs. I didn't care about anything." Dakota shook his head. "I have no clue why I was acting like that. I felt like someone else."

Laughing, Noah replied. "Well, when men get around women, we are different."

"She was more than a woman. It was like she wasn't even human."

"Oh, she was mortal. She was probably nuts. I mean, how many women are out there in a sports car cruising the highways for a twenty-five-year-old rez kid?"

Dakota tilted his head to the side. "I know it sounds bizarre, but that was exactly what she was doing. She told me when she became lonely and couldn't sleep; she would go for a ride. I asked her if she was scared a killer would find her and she giggled. I could see she had no fear." Looking at Noah out of the corner of his eye, he went on. "She shifted closer to my seat as I drove and asked me if I was dangerous."

Noah's eyes grew large. "Oh, shit. Did you make out with a strange woman?"

"I couldn't help it. She was all over me. I thought I would wreck. Instead, I felt super focused."

"You mean you were driving with her touching you?"

Dakota's eyes glazed over. "Yeah, it was like magic."

Noah couldn't explain it, but concern was filling his senses. He had never seen his brother disoriented and distracted. Dakota was talking like he was going insane. "Um, Dakota, where is this girl? Why didn't she stay with you?"

Dakota looked around. "I don't know. I begged her to stay, but she said she had to go home. I asked her if she had a curfew and she laughed. She said it was something like that." Drawing a deep breath, Dakota blew air into his cheeks as he exhaled. "I've been sitting here on the porch since she took off. I just can't get her out of my mind. I feel like I need to go find her, but I don't know where to look."

Considering everything Dakota had told him, Noah rubbed his palms together. "Look, man. She was just cruising for a piece. That's how those wealthy women are. She was bored with her husband and went looking for a young guy. Right now, she is sneaking in the front door of her mansion. She won't ever think of you again." Noah shook his head. "You always do this. You mix up sex and love. You're not in love, baby brother. She was just experienced. I have been with those kinds of women. They are fun, but they go home to their husbands. I mean, you'll be the talk of her next girls' night out and then that'll be it."

Dakota looked down at his feet as he nodded his head. "It felt so real. It felt like she was actually into me."

Noah placed his hand on Dakota's shoulder. "That's what they do. Those cougars are skilled predators disguised as bored housewives."

"I guess so, but I will never forget this. I may not have known her name, but I will never forget her face. She was so beautiful."

"I know, man. At least you still have me." Noah grinned.

Dakota shrugged his shoulders and grinned. "Well, I suppose there is that. You don't look as hot as her, though."

"Ha! I hope not. Our neighbor over there keeps staring at my long native hair like he wants to roll in it naked."

"I think that guy definitely has a crush on you." Dakota's laugh faded. "I guess she isn't coming back, huh?"

Becoming serious, Noah shook his head. "Nah, she's long gone." Noah poked Dakota with his elbow. "I got a six-pack in my truck. Want to split it?"

"Yeah, I guess. I'll go to bed after a few beers. I feel drained."

Noah stood from his seat on the porch step and shuffled down the steps. As he rummaged through his cooler in his truck, he spoke to Dakota over his shoulder. "Maybe we can go fishing later. I heard they were biting at Uncle Jack's Pond. We could have a traditional fish fry or something. What do you say?"

As Noah dug through the thawed ice, he noticed Dakota wasn't answering. He glanced over his shoulder. Dakota looked like a pale ghost as he watched his brother. Noah drew his hand out of the cooler. "Hey, on second thought, why don't you go to bed? You don't look so hot."

Dakota's tone sounded as if he were in a stupor as he responded. "Yeah, maybe you're right. I feel depleted. It has been a long night."

As Noah walked towards the porch, he watched Dakota stand from his seat. Dakota turned toward the front door. Terror washed over Noah as the streetlight illuminated Dakota's body. Deep puncture wounds were on the side of Dakota's neck. Noah ran to his brother. "What the hell happened?"

Dakota stared at Noah. "Huh?"

"Your neck! Oh, my God!" Noah placed his palm over the weeping gash. "You've been bitten! Did that woman bite you?"

Dakota lifted his hand to his neck. He wiped blood from his skin. He then looked at his hand with bewilderment. "I don't know. I can't remember anything after she crawled into my lap."

"We gotta get you to the emergency room!" Noah grabbed Dakota by the arm and led him to his truck. His mind raced. "How could I have left him at that party? My booze caused this! I'm so stupid," Noah thought to himself.

Noah vowed from that night on he would never let Dakota walk those darkened streets. They never spoke of that night again.

Dakota thought about the mystery woman and if she was out there waiting for him. She was dangerous. She had changed him. He craved her blood, and he fought every single day to not kill his brother or any of the other innocent people on the reservation. He needed to find the mystery woman soon. The Park Rangers were noticing the shortage of animals in the mountains.

He knew he was a monster, but that didn't stop Dakota from wanting another midnight ride.

Quarantine

Day 1.

Hi, my name is Danny. Gosh, that sounds stupid. I have never written in a journal before, so I am not sure how this works. If I wasn't alone in this house, I know someone would snicker at the paradox of my last remark. See, I'm an author. An author of what you ask? Well... a little of everything, but mostly horror. I'm not on any top seller's list, but so far, I have had a pretty good run with my book sales. Ten years ago, I thought I had to work for a publishing company to succeed as a writer. Thanks to modern technology, I can upload my books to online bookstores. Eh, publisher shmublisher. I get along just fine without them.

My grandpa, who was also a writer, would have laughed in my face. He would drone on at how easy I have it compared to his past as a writer. I don't really care what a dead man would think of my way of life. I'm too old to care what that stale old bastard would have thought. So why did I mention it? Who the hell knows?

Why am I writing in a journal, you ask? Today is my first day living through an international quarantine. A virus broke out. I can't even pronounce its name. So far, it's wreaked havoc all over the world. It started in a little town halfway across the world. Funny thing, I can't remember the name of the place.

Since the outbreak, fingers are pointing on all sides at each other. I can't say that I am shocked. A week ago, the news warned us this pathogen was coming. They suggested we should go to the stores to stock up on supplies. I'm not much of a people person. I went online and made an order at my local grocery store. Being a hermit has its advantages. I knew precisely what items I needed to purchase and how much. That was my routine before the virus. I shopped from home every week. When I went to pick up my order, it didn't look like people were concerned. The store operated as usual in its regular hours of operation. After the Sunny Mart worker loaded up fifty bags into my trunk, he threw me a "what the hell" look before he left. Trust me, I'm used to it. The CDC said to have a month's worth of food and supplies. I bought two months, just in case. I hope it blows over before I run out.

Day 2.

So far, being shut in is not too bad. I'm used to the routine of being alone. I do my work when most people are mindlessly watching television, but today, I feel distracted. I peeked out the window today, and it looked like the neighbors were grilling out. Of course, I'm not invited. Why, you ask? I am a hermit. Didn't you read the first entry? Sure, I would love to eat one of their hotdogs or maybe sample Mrs. Johnson's baked beans. It wouldn't work out however, I never could stand being around people longer than it would take to eat that hotdog and baked beans. What would be left? Mindless conversation about subjects I hate to talk about or concerns I can't relate to. Don't forget about the unwanted arrival of gas created by

Mrs. Johnson's baked beans. I've experienced moments like that. Trust me, it ain't pretty.

The Johnson's have two kids. I have never been in a relationship for more than a month. Kids never happened to me. Women like to go out a lot. You may have predicted my response to that. It's a one-way street, mainly for her. I have had a few online relationships, if you want to call them that.

The relationships would be short-lived. There would be a few deep stories exchanged, and maybe a few x-rated phone calls would be made. Then they too would become restless and block me from their social media. They wanted better than what I could give them; they needed to meet face to face. I couldn't do it. It didn't hurt me. I felt relief instead. Weird, huh? I don't know why I wrote about that stuff. I guess the pandemic makes a guy regret a few things. I could have tried harder. Maybe I wouldn't be alone right now.

None of it compares to my life now.

Day 3.

I checked the news online and the stores are running out of food. That was quick. What a difference forty-eight hours can make during a pandemic. First it was the bread, and then the meat. Now, the people are getting into street fights over toilet paper. Toilet paper? Really? I thought the snow preppers were bad, but this is taking on an unusual shade of ugly.

I peeked out the window again today. Mr. and Mrs. Johnson were loading their children into their soccer-mom van. I'm guessing they're heading to the store. Fool thing to do right now if you ask me.

My neighbors, the Crowley's, across the road are at least eighty. They seem to be relaxed about the whole thing. Mr. Crowley is on his riding lawnmower, smoking a cigarette. He has been riding that tractor since the sunlight touched his grass. It's driving me up the wall with the noise. Nothing is worse to an author than to be disturbed by a noise you can't shut out. His grass doesn't need to be cut. I think it's just an excuse to ride around his yard to avoid his wife. Mrs. Crowley was snapping beans on their front porch, giving him the evil eye.

Day 4.

The news broadcast this morning that the governor has declared a state of emergency. He ordered all businesses to shut down for a month. I'm uncertain how I should feel about that, but I am prepared; at least I think I am.

I put on a mask and strolled out to my mailbox. Hey, you can't be too careful. I mean… what if this thing is airborne? Anyway, as I trudged to my mailbox, I couldn't help but note how eerily quiet my street had become overnight. This time of day, I normally heard the automobiles on the highway or the tourist train making their daily trip to a nearby town. Today, I overheard Mr. and Mrs. Johnson fighting. I couldn't understand precisely what they were saying, but I picked up words. It sounded like they were blaming each other for something. I snatched my newspaper and power walked back into the safety of my home.

Day 5.

I hate to admit it, but I am bored. I have been working on a story about aliens. Yeah, I know, but I'm into it. I usually woke up, had my coffee, and later I would write. That has regularly been my routine; until now. I peered into that white glowing sheet of virtual paper until my eyeballs were ready to drop out of my head. Nothing would come to me. I seldom experience writer's block.

I think it has something to do with this quarantine. One of my methods, if I became mentally clogged, I would go for a stroll in the park. The government closed the parks last night.

I don't understand how walking outside could make people sick. Apparently, they see something I don't. I guess I am royally screwed. I can see the neighbors are feeling the pressure, too.

Looking out the window has developed into a major pass time for me. Mr. and Mrs. Johnson are presently sitting on their porch smoking pot while they watch Mr. Crowley ride around in circles in his yard. Did I mention his yard measures only a quarter of an acre? I kid you not. But he mows that portion of dirt like a champ. Mrs. Crowley is on the porch once again, giving her husband a nasty look. This time, however, she ain't snapping beans.

Day 6

I didn't bother to sit at my computer until I was ready to write my journal entry. The concepts for my novel just won't come. My creative writing teacher told me you can't force a turd. So instead of inviting my eyeballs to jump out of their sockets, I sat by my window. I sipped my coffee and observed my neighbors. I don't dare to go outside. It is getting weird out there. The Johnson's fought all night, and the police came. They removed the children from the house.

The entire neighborhood stood outside and watched the action. Even Mr. Crowley came out of his house to watch the spectacle unfold. The faces of the people gawking at the Johnson's proved they simply wanted to know what was going on. They didn't want to help the people they lived next to. Why would they? They needed to worry about their own households; right?

Day 7

Today, I watched ten fire trucks rush by my house. Someone set fire to the local library. It made me sick to my stomach someone could do such a thing. All those books… gone. The police have been patrolling the streets. They've been talking through speakers mounted on top of their patrol cars. I threw on a mask and leaned my head out the door to hear what one of them said. They were ordering everybody to stay home and to not leave their neighborhoods. They didn't say as much, but the severe tone they used sounded like a threat. I must admit it. I am feeling frightened.

I have written about situations where martial law was activated, but this isn't one of my books. This wasn't about aliens, zombies, or World War three. This is real… this is real.

Day 8

My hands are shaking as I write today's entry. The President enacted martial law. The police are now demanding we stay in our homes. I watched news footage of the military firing upon American citizens with rubber bullets. My mind is struggling to comprehend what I am seeing. Towns are on fire; bodies are piling up in the streets and in the morgues. Refrigerated trucks are on standby at the hospitals to accommodate all the bodies.

The people are going crazy all around me. They are breaking into stores and cars. Entire cities are on fire. I can see the smoke from my window. The sirens are growing closer every minute.

Day 9

You won't believe what transpired this morning. I sat by my window with my morning coffee. Mr. Crowley started up his mower. Nothing surprising there. He climbed aboard with his cigarette lit between his lips. Next, he started his usual laps around his tiny yard. I chuckled at the balls the elderly man had to disregard the stay inside order.

Mr. Crowley smirked as he passed his wife loop after loop as she remained on the porch watching him. Mrs. Crowley stood on the deck for what seemed like an eternity. The hostility in the air was building like bricks in a high-rise hotel. I assumed she had given up on her crusade to persuade Mr. Crowley to stop the lawnmower. Her face dissolved into a grin, and she twisted around and went into the house. I smiled to myself at the loving exchange. Five minutes later, however, Mrs. Crowley came out the front door with a double-barreled shotgun. I nearly pissed my pants as I dropped my scalding hot coffee on my lap. I rose to my feet and banged on my window. Mr. Crowley couldn't hear me. I needed to reach for my phone, but everything was happening too fast.

Mr. Crowley took a left turn towards his house. His eyes bulged out of his head when he saw his wife with the shotgun. He dove off his lawn mower and rolled into the grass. I looked on with panic as Mr. Crowley jumped to his feet and dashed towards the street. The lawn mower kept moving behind him until it ran into the side of the house. Mrs. Crowley laughed like a wicked witch as she jumped from the porch. She cleared five steps without tumbling to the ground. Her pink curlers in her hair bounced, and her pink bathrobe flew behind her as she raced after her husband. She ran fast for an eighty-year-old woman. It was as if pure rage was giving her superpowers.

Mr. Crowley screamed for someone to call the police and for someone to help him. You guessed it; no one came. Mrs. Crowley made her way out into the road and opened both barrels into her husband's back. His face froze as the life drained out of him.

You know what was strange? Other than my old fart neighbor killing her husband? Mr. Crowley looked over at me as the air escaped his body. He smirked one last time before he hit the ground.

Go figure that one out.

Day 10

I'm half a sleep as I journal this morning. I lingered by my window all night. It took the police until after dark to come to my street. I sat and watched Mrs. Crowley as she sat next to her husband's body. She placed his head in her lap and combed his hair with her fingertips. I could see she loved him, but she didn't regret what she did. The neighborhood was too frightened to approach her. She still had her shotgun beside of her. When the police showed up, a stand-off happened until dawn. Every time a police officer tried to approach her; she placed her hand on her gun. Exhausted, the police decided enough was enough.

The Sheriff walked cautiously towards Mrs. Crowley with his palms in the air to show he wasn't a threat. My heart dropped as I watched her seize her shotgun and point it at the police officer. Ten officers discharged their firearms into her frail body. I puked on my window...

Day 11

No coffee this morning. I couldn't face the prospect of anything touching my stomach. Having to wash the dried vomit off my window this morning was no cakewalk. Aw... damn. Cake...

Day 12

After my unwelcome puke fest yesterday, I woke up and inhaled a breakfast that could choke a pig. I finished my meal by devouring an entire pot of coffee. As I drained my fourth cup, I sat by my window. The military is now patrolling the streets of my town and neighborhood. They are wearing riot gear and gasmask. The recording playing from their tanks is saying they are firing with real bullets and to remain inside. I don't know why, but it made me melancholy to watch the soldiers stomp over Mr. Crowley's bloodstain on the road with their boots.

Day 13

Last night, an alarm bell interrupted my program I was watching on television. A voice chimed in after the bell had become silent. I felt my blood drain from my face as the voice spoke my name. It informed me the government had selected me because I was a writer. It said to gather only what I could carry on my back and to be ready to be escorted by the military to a new location. I don't have time to write any more. I can hear the trucks coming.

Week 10

I guess you noticed I couldn't write to you. I am not allowed to address the details of where I am. It was the condition they allowed me if I wished to keep my computer.

It's silly how much I had become reliant on my journal. It comforted me through an extraordinary time in our history as humans. Funny sentence to say, seeing that I am now lulled to sleep by the sound of bombs dropping above ground.

I don't know what is happening out there, other than the government is slaughtering millions. I don't know how all of this started or if it will end. All I know is that I live underground, and I document everything the government instructs me to write. I was one of twenty writers that were saved from the catastrophe above me.

This happened.

This is happening.

I have not written one story since this began.

After all, reality is scarier than my fiction.

Creeker Hollow

Some claim there are more things in the world unseen than seen. Bumps in the night and shadows that move without sound, soul, or purpose. Have you felt a presence in the darkness as you lay comfortably in your bed? Maybe you heard a piercing scream outside your window. Did you dare get up and investigate? Were you brave enough to ask, "What do you want?"

I never imagined someone like me would be that guy. I'm a plain country boy from Mudsuck, West Virginia. Never have I been the brave soul that would dare to ask questions. I lived my life. I went to my shitty job during day, had a few beers at night, rinsed and repeated the next day. Maybe I was bored, or I didn't give a damn anymore, but one day I asked questions.

Talk about stupid…

To begin my strange tale, I think I should give you an understanding of where I live. Mudsuck is an old hollow, or as my grandmother pronounced it, holler. Don't search for it on a map, you won't find it. My Grandmother is a descendant of the English pioneers who settled here before the civil war. She rarely speaks of the past, and she is the last elder in our hollow that knows the complete history of the pioneers.

There isn't much to Mudsuck. We have a Sheriff and a deputy with a one cell jailhouse. We have a post office big enough for three people at a time. There are four paved roads to our town, and they all circle back to the city hall. The rest of the roads are composed of dirt and gravel. The twist and turns of the dirt roads could break a snake's back. Hell, you could break your neck if you look off at the wrong time.

We have one gas station and a drive-in restaurant. The drive-in is where the teenagers hang out. As a teen, you either went to the drive-in or the swimming hole in the summer. The drive-in played the latest music and had the best hamburgers in the world. Occasionally, we would see a few teenagers from the rich side of town. We called them the hillers. They were the wealthy kids that lived in the hills of Charleston. It was an upscale suburb where the physicians and lawyers lived. While the Mudsuck kids drove bombs, the hillers drove their daddy's Mercedes. The hillers went to the drive-in to make fun of us. They laughed about our hand-me- down clothes, and our ability to afford a hamburger from the drive in. Yeah, a lot of fights took place at the drive-in.

Oh… and did I mention that once a month the entire town disappears? Yeah, you heard me right. One night out of the month, on the full moon, the people of Mudsuck and their children hide. For an entire night, we hunker down in the basements of our homes. We pray for the sunrise to return, and for the ground to stop shaking. As far back as I can remember, this has been my way of life.

Do I have your attention yet?

I asked Grandma to tell me what the noise was outside. I begged her to explain why the ground shuddered. Grandma, with a delicate tone, would instruct me to close my eyes and continue praying. After everyone fell asleep,

I would remain awake. I struggled to guess at what could cause the ground shake. My best friend John told me to quit trying to make trouble for our families. He would tell me to shut up and go to sleep. If he knew me, he would realize I was the type of guy that would never shut up and pray. Like I mentioned, it was boredom or not giving a damn. I couldn't determine which. I had an abrupt impulse to know what forced the town to hide. I decided on the next full moon I would find out what the mystery was, even if it killed me.

Grandma was on her front porch snapping beans for supper. Her weathered hands were skilled in preparing food that would melt in your mouth. I sat at her feet on the hardwood. The evening sun beat down on my face. Grandma hummed a tune I had never heard before. I felt my body relaxing. I cherished those moments with her. She was the closest thing I had to a mother. My mother died in childbirth and my dad had disappeared before I was born. Grandma took me in and raised me. I feel lucky about that.

"Richard?"

"Hum?" I answered drowsily.

"What are you pondering about over there? I can hear the wheels spinning." She said as she grinned and tossed another snapped bean into her basin.

"I was just thinking about the full moon."

Grandma stiffened in her rocking chair. She hated it when I brought up the nights with the full moon. "What do you want to know this time, Richard? You know I don't like this subject."

"I just need to know what the quake is and why it happens to us."

Grandma stopped rocking in her chair. She set her basin of beans on the porch beside her chair. She arranged her hands on her lap and peered into the setting sun. "Richard, you realize I am an elderly woman. I don't plan on living forever. There are stories that were passed down to me when I was a little girl. My Grandmother told me the tale and her mother told her. It's a tradition in my family. I consider it a gift and a burden to know these stories. Your mother was the one that I was to pass the stories down to and… you know the rest." Grandma picked up the corner of her apron and swabbed at the corner of her eye. "I sure miss her."

"I know, Grandma." I replied as I patiently waited for her to begin again. I never knew my mother. I couldn't share in her mourning.

"When I was a little girl here in the holler, I recall being scared. I could hear the running of the horses." Grandma glanced at me from the corner of her eye.

Smiling at my expression, Grandma went on. "Oh yes, they are ghost horses. I was told there are two hundred of them."

"But… why? I mean…" I stammered as I mopped the perspiration from my brow. I ransacked my brain for logical reasons. Why would ghost horses run through our little hole-in-the-wall town?

"I realize it's hard to believe. But it's true. I recall one night when I was ten years old. I was sleepwalking. Somehow, I let myself out of the cellar. As I cleared the door to go outside, my mother caught the back of my nightgown. It woke me from my sleep. I woke up as she was closing the door, and that's when I saw them."

"You saw the horses?"

"Yes, I saw them, but merely for a second. After that, I was too anxious to sleep. It scared me I might sleepwalk. I never wished to look at those creatures again." Grandma said no more, but you can believe it, I was going to go look. Now that I had found out about this piece of information, the urge became an obsession. The full moon was taking place the next night. Before Grandma finished her story, I already had a plan worked up in my mind.

"Hey Grandma, I'm going to John's house tomorrow night. He's having a sleepover with a couple of buddies. His mom said they had room for me in their cellar."

"Well… I suppose that would be ok. Make sure you call me when the sun comes up. I want to make certain you're ok."

And that, ladies and gentlemen, was how I ended up in the wood's half a mile from my grandmother's house. Lighting up a cigarette, I squat down beside the fattest tree I could find. I wanted to hide from the ghost horses. I couldn't believe I was doing it. What if they kill me? Can they kill me?

I pressed the tiny button on my wristwatch. The green glow said it was eleven fifty-nine, October thirty-first. It was a full moon on Halloween. I sure could pick them. Who else would dare go out on Halloween? Dumbass me, that's who. I sucked down the last of my cigarette with a shaking hand before I snuffed it out with my foot. The green glow of my watch turned itself off. It left me in the dark once more. My heart pounded against my ribs. I thought it would erupt out of my flannel shirt. I rubbed my chest, thinking it would help. It beat harder.

The blood drained out of my body as I felt the first tremors beneath my feet. I stretched out my hand against the bark. I leaned around the tree just enough to see the dirt road in front of me. The rumble was growing louder by the second. I gripped the tree bark tighter, as if it could shield me. I could sense they were close. They were inches from making their appearance. I dug my nails into the bark of the tree in anticipation. Then it happened.

It was as if it were taking place in slow motion. A strange fog rolled in. The fog stuck to the ground as if it were preparing a new road just for the horses. And suddenly I saw it, transparent hooves rounding the corner. My frightened eyes observed the magnificent steed's bodies up to their gigantic heads. There were too many to count. The horses' ghostly bodies glistened with perspiration. Their flesh looked to be in a state of decomposition, with bones protruding through their rotting skin. Their eyes were the palest white that I had ever seen. I could see their breath leaving their nostrils in the crisp October air as they pounded their mangled hooves against the ground.

Grandma left out one detail, or maybe she didn't see them. There were riders on those horses. They looked half man, half animal, with their faces painted in intricate patterns. They screamed unnatural sounds as they twirled sticks with curious objects dangling from the ends. It looked like decayed feathers and rotting turtle shells.

As they passed me, I noticed an ancient smell. It was primitive and musky, with a hint of burning timber. It burned my nose and my eyes, but I resisted the urge to blink. My eyes were watering, but I couldn't look away. I watched as the horses and their riders stormed past me.

Hooves hammered against the earth. Still, they left no disturbance on the ground.

My heart fell as I realized the last horse had just filed past me. It couldn't end there. I had to follow. Slithering like a snake from behind my tree, I ran behind the ghost riders and their ghostly steeds. The thunder of the horse's hooves drowned out my intense, laborious breathing. They rode to creeker hollow and into a field toward a towering oak tree. The town had named it Lonesome Oak field. I paused and stared as the phantom riders kept up their incessant screaming. It was as if they never ran out of breath.

Abandoning my rational judgment, I crept through the open field. No longer did I care if they could detect my existence at any moment. My brain raced with insanity as I sought to catch up with them. I stopped once again in my tracks as I witnessed an amazing sight. The ghost riders ran straight for the oak tree. They didn't just run toward the oak; they passed through the oak tree. Not one rider appeared out of the other side. My mind raced with a thousand questions. I almost turned to flee when one of the ghost riders broke loose and rounded to face me.

My knees locked into place. I realized at that point they had noticed my presence. Was this the moment I would lose my head to a ghost? For some unknown reason, I didn't care. I just needed to find out what the ghost rider had in mind for me. My heart felt like it was pounding out its last pulses. My limbs were swaying beneath me. They were ordering me to run, but I just couldn't do it. The ghost rider kicked the sides of the rotting horse beneath his body. He leaned forward with the horse to urge him to go faster. I couldn't blink… I couldn't even scream.

The stallion's nostrils flared as its mane fluttered in the breezeless night. The ghost rider shouted and whirled his rotten stick as he charged towards me. I had no means to defend myself. It felt foolish, but it was the only thing that came to mind. I flung my hands in the air in surrender and screamed. "I'm sorry! I'm sorry!" I said as I stood with my hands in the air like a cowboy in a black and white movie.

The ghost rider came within inches of my body as he came to a halt. The decaying spotted horse blew its frigid breath into my face. Raising my eyes to the ghost rider, I repeated the sentiment again, but not as loud. "I'm sorry." I don't know why, but my eyes picked this moment to well up with tears. The ghost rider stared at me with soulless black eyes. He dismounted from his horse and walked up to me. He had long, flowing raven black hair. A pendant composed of bone and turquoise hung around his neck. His clothing was made of crumbling brown leather. Risking a glance at his feet, I noted they were bare and soiled with dirt.

I kept my hands in the air as he walked a complete circle around me. He brushed his chilly hand across my hair. As he came around to my front, he stepped closer to me. His breath was icy against my flesh and smelled rich with sweetgrass. I jumped as he spoke to me. His language was something I had never heard before. He paused in mid-sentence and stared at me. He tried again. "Your language is English. Yes?" His voice was smooth, deep and hollow.

"Yes, sir." I stuttered.

"Why do you follow us this night?"

"I was tired of being scared."

"You are afraid?" The phantom replied with a hint of astonishment in his tone.

"Yes, sir, terrified, sir." I felt like a child frightened by a schoolteacher.

"You said, I am sorry?"

"Yes, sir."

The ghost rider nodded his head. "Then it is finished." The ghost turned and mounted his horse. As he glanced down at me, I noticed his eyes had changed from black to a soft chestnut. "Thank you." He said as he pulled on the horse's mane. He swung the horse around and headed to the oak tree. Before he disappeared; he twisted around and gave a slight wave. As he turned to go into the lonesome oak, I noticed he and his horse no longer looked decayed. They looked peaceful and whole.

I remained long after he vanished, like an idiot, with my hands in the air. I stood there until my knees buckled and I crumpled to the ground.

The frosty grass with its wet dew soaked through my blue jeans and woke me from my stupor. I glanced around. The sun was rising. I had survived the night. I saw the ghost horses and their riders.

After everything that took place, I had questions that needed to be resolved. They were questions only my grandmother could answer. She held out on me, and it was time for her to fess up.

I ran as fast as I could through the field. My lungs burned from the strain as I rushed through the woods to my grandmother's house. As I stumbled onto her front lawn, the sun was cresting over the mountainside. Her front door burst open as she ran, shouting and wailing. She dashed over to me with her arms wide. She grabbed me and yanked me into a bear hug. I could scarcely breathe. "Richard! Oh, my Richard! I called over to John's house! He said he did not know what I was talking about when I mentioned the sleepover! Oh, Richard, why? Why would you do this to me?" She wept like a child on my shoulder. In all my twenty years of living as her child, I had never witnessed tears such as these.

"I'm sorry, Grandma. I'm sorry. Really, I am. Come on now, don't cry. I had to see the horses."

Grandma stopped sobbing, and she stared at me with panic. "You did what?"

"I had to see the horses, Grandma. It was… it was… amazing!" I said as I scanned her tear-streaked face for a reaction. Instead, she caught my hand and led me to the porch. I helped her to rest her shaking body in her rocking chair. Next, I sat on the step at her feet. "Please, Grandma. Tell me the truth. You left out the riders on the horses."

Grandma wiped her eyes with a wrinkled tissue she had retrieved from her shirt pocket. "Yes… I left out something. I'm sorry. I could have gotten you killed. I did not know you would go searching for them." She replied as she sniffed and wiped her nose. "Well, the legend goes like this. It was during the civil war; the Indians were all over these lands. Before this was West Virginia, this was the home of the Seneca. Our ancestors had just arrived from England. They fell in love with this area. They went to the government to eradicate the land of the barbarians so they could settle there. One horrible action after another followed, and they carried out a gruesome choice and… oh, Richard."

A whimper swelled in my grandmother's throat as she pressed on. "The army wiped the entire Seneca village out. Countless warriors, women, and children perished. The

Seneca warriors left behind fought for three blood filled days and nights. They too fell one by one until their leader stood alone. On the third night, the full moon was shining where my house sits. The warrior thrust his arms up and yelled. He vowed they would return someday and take their homeland back. He wailed at the moon and begged the Great Spirit to accompany him in his quest. The soldiers shot him."

Grandma sniffed and dried her eyes again. "The worst is yet to be told. They burned their village to the ground. Our ancestors whistled and sang merry tunes as if it was a celebration. They stepped over the bodies to choose where their homes would be built. After a few hours had passed, they gathered up the remains of the once beautiful Seneca people. They took them to Lonesome Oak field, dug an enormous grave and shoved them in there as if they were worth nothing. Our forefathers didn't want it recorded in the history books about what they had done, so they planted an oak tree over the gravesite to mark the sight. I suppose they assumed the story would end there, but it didn't."

My grandmother stared at me with watery eyes. "My great-great grandma was there. She witnessed these events, and she knew it was nothing more than murder. She passed the story along and well… there you have it. The curse of creeker holler started on the next full moon. It scared the settlers the Seneca would avenge their dead. They built cellars and established the ritual of hiding every full moon. I know they regretted what they did, but it was too late to take it back. No one knew how to make it right."

"Wow; it all makes sense now." I told Grandma of what transpired that night. We both decided that my gesture of surrender and my apology saved my life.

As the months went by and we gathered in our cellars to pray, the horses never appeared again. Grandma and I guessed I had somehow made peace with the Seneca. How do you explain that to a bunch of frightened town folk? How do you explain the nightmare is over? You can't. Grandma and I kept it to ourselves.

I can say now that I am a genuine believer in the unseen. Now, I wonder what else is out there. If ghost are real, what does that mean about the other things that go bump in the night?

Dare I ask those questions again?

Will I search for answers?

Maybe…

Atticus

Jason walked through his cramped trailer sweating bullets. He was determined to quit drinking this time. It was late fall outside. Inside his body, however, it felt like the third circle of hell was boiling just under his skin. He looked at his wristwatch for the hundredth time. He tried to sober up many times before, failing miserably. After every bender, he would say it was the last one. Then something would happen at work, his car would break down, his ex would demand more money, and bills would be too high. It wouldn't take much to make him say "To hell with it", and rush to the store to pick up a twelve pack of beer.

Walking over to the window, Jason gazed into the sunset in the distance. He knew sobering up this time was not an option. He would lose everything if he couldn't get that drink out of his life. His supervisor smelled stale alcohol on his breath for the last time. Next time, they would fire him. Today was the first time he wished he were a wealthy man. If he was rich, he could afford a fancy rehab where they dope you up and call you a good boy when it's all over.

"Why did I pick today?" Jason whispered to himself. "I can't quit cold turkey. What if I have a seizure like that guy on the news? Look at me, I'm already sweating like it's the middle of July and..." Jason laughed to himself. "And look at me. I'm talking to myself already. Thank God my mom is not around to witness this."

Jason stepped over to the refrigerator and opened the door. The cold air rushed over his face as he considered the food Zoe had brought over the weekend before. He rolled his eyes with annoyance. They had an intoxicated one-night stand, and now she thought they were in a relationship. Jason couldn't figure out why she would choose him as a boyfriend. He was no prize. He would let everyone down if he was allowed the opportunity. His mother repeatedly instructed him, "don't shit where you eat". Jason laughed to himself sarcastically. "That's what you get, old man. You screwed a co-worker. You should've taken mom's advice."

Anger filled his heart. The one thing he needed the most was not in the refrigerator. He flung the door shut and cussed under his breath. His throat blazed with the desire for the ice-cold beer to run down and put out the flame. His heart pounded inside his ribcage with yearning. He paced back and forth like a caged lion.

The urge became too much. Jason ran to the bathroom cabinet and drew out a prescription the doctor gave him the last time he landed himself in the E. R. The physician informed him the tablets would protect him from experiencing delirium tremens also known as DT's. It took him three days to understand the pills were for alcoholics. Until he went to the hospital for alcohol poisoning, he never considered himself an alcoholic.

Jason hated to do it, but he felt desperate. He didn't want to admit it frightened him he could die. He constantly told himself he was a waste of space, and the world wouldn't notice his absence. Believing he deserved death, he drank with reckless abandon since he was a teenager. It surprised him he wanted to live.

With blurry vision, Jason narrowed his eyes to read the directions on the bottle. All he could make out was the word "two". He shrugged his shoulders. "Take two and call me in the morning." He said with a heavy sigh.

His sweaty hands trembled as he twisted off the cap. He slipped his finger into the vial and brought out two glossy white tablets. He shoved them into his mouth. Turning the knob on the waterspout, Jason cupped his hand and gathered water. He raised his hand to his mouth and swallowed the pills. Hands shaking, he replaced the cap onto the bottle. He stuffed the bottle into his pocket for later.

The floor appeared to be moving into an upward angle. Jason gripped the sides of the sink to steady himself. He glanced up into the mirror. Fear ripped through his soul as he stared into the face of a man that he no longer recognized. He followed a bead of sweat as it made a trail from his gaunt forehead, down his boney cheek and as it slipped across his parched, cracked lips. A lump swelled in his throat. "How could that be the same man that once had it all?" Jason thought to himself. "I had a wife, kids and a great job. Now, I am about to lose my career."

Standing straight, Jason stepped away from the afflicted stranger in the mirror. He made his way to the living room and sat on the couch. He turned on the television for comfort. Every channel was saturated with digital snow. Flipping through the empty channels, he hoped to find something that would give him company through the night. There had to be a channel that could fill the desolate void that was all around him. He eventually settled on a channel that was full of squiggly lines. "At least I can listen to the

local broadcast." Jason said to himself as he tossed the re-
mote control onto the coffee table.

As he listened to the reporters repeat the same stories
of traffic accidents, weather and drama over and over, he
felt the medicine kicking in. His body eased, and he felt
sleepy for the first time in years. He set his head backward
against the cushioned sofa and drifted off to sleep.

Loud barking jolted through Jason's body and awak-
ened him with a start. He raised his head as the barking
and growling became stronger and louder. He stood up and
stepped over to the window. It was too dark to see past his
front porch. Jason could feel his temper rising at the dog's
persistent barking. He moved to the front door and opened
it. He strode outside and yelled into the dark. "Shut up!" Jason grinned at the abrupt quiet brought on by his outburst.
It felt satisfying to yell. He needed to yell at something. A
big mouth dog was as good of a reason as any.

"Damn dog." Jason said to himself as he twisted to go
back inside. He closed the door behind him. As he turned
around, terror engulfed him. He stood face to face with the
most hideous dog he had ever seen. Was it even a dog? It
was unlike a typical dog. Its skin was crumpled and looked
to be made of grey ashes. When it moved, some of those
ashes fell to the floor like an extreme case of dandruff. His
massive paws made no noise as he crept towards Jason's
frail body. The evil hound's eyes were a greenish gold that
smoldered behind his heavy eyelids. Ashy skin wrinkled
around his yellow, jagged teeth. The dog growled, a pro-
foundly sinister noise from deep within his tarnished body.

Jason knew in his diminished state he was no match
for the enormous animal in front of him. He took baby

steps backward towards the door. Reaching the door, he felt around for the doorknob. The dog saw what he was about to do. It lunged to attack, but Jason dodged out of the way. Instead of crashing into the door, the dog passed through the solid wood. Was it a phantom of Jason's imagination? Jason stood gawking at the door, shuddering from the shock of the bizarre incident. His heart pounded faster as he listened to the dog outside barking and growling for his attention once more. He was cornered, no doubt about that. Jason realized he would have to confront the dog and maybe end its life.

Jason went to the window, mopped the perspiration from his forehead, and peeked outside. The hound was lingering on the porch. Jason slapped the window with his hand. "Leave me alone, you dumb dog!"

The dog ignored Jason's request and instead, he coiled up on the porch. It kept its eyes on Jason; never once did it blink. "What is he waiting for?" Jason thought as he tiptoed away from the window to search for a weapon. As he glanced around his empty trailer, he regretted pawning his guns for beer. He scanned around the living room and located a bat propped in the corner. It was the only gift his old man had given him when he was a little boy. He stepped over to the corner and seized the end of the bat. He grasped the polished wood in his right hand. Turning around, he strode to the front door. He opened the door with his free hand.

The dog stood up, turned away, and walked off the porch. He shifted toward the darkness and wandered into the woods. The dog paused, turned, and stood by for Jason to follow. Jason knew it was foolish, but there was something oddly familiar about that creature. Hoping curiosity wouldn't drive him to an uncertain demise, Jason closed his eyes. He spoke a brief prayer to himself before opening his eyes and heading down the steps. His limbs shook underneath him as he shuffled towards the waiting dog. He clutched his bat tight in his hand as he pushed forward.

As Jason got closer, the dog turned and wandered further into the woods. Jason knew those woods like the back of his hand. He was born and raised in those woods. Heck, his family had been there for generations. He knew the passage in front of him completely. Surprise filled his senses as he noticed the dog walking towards his mother's former home. She had passed ten years ago. Jason knew from all the years he had wandered up there, his mother's residence should have been more run-down. If Jason didn't know better, he would have thought he stepped back in time.

The cabin looked as if it had recently been built, but that was impossible. The last time Jason looked at the cabin, the roof was collapsing, and the front porch had a hole in it. Now, it was as if time had never disturbed it. The dog sat like a trained house pet and stared at the house. Jason kept a forceful grip on his bat as he stepped closer to the house. He held the dog in his sights as he strode up the steps onto the porch. He took one last glimpse over at the dog sitting in the grass, watching him.

Satisfied the dog would not charge him; he twisted and peered into the window. Grief and confusion washed over him as he looked at his mother sitting at the kitchen table. She was scribbling on a scrap of stationery and smoking a cigarette.

Jason looked on with wonder at his beautiful mother. It was years before the cancer, and before the doctors carved a gigantic crater in her throat, hoping to spare her life. He wanted to rush in there and take that cigarette out of her hand and beg her to quit. There were no words to express how alone he had been since she died. She had been his best friend through many tough times. To surrender her to cancer was the worst thing that had ever happened to him.

Jason watched as she put out her cigarette, stood up, and grabbed her coat. Her soft voice called out. "Jason! I'm leaving for the grocery store. Do you want to go?" She asked as she took her list and crammed into her dress pocket. Jason was cemented to the window as his fourteen-year-old self came around the corner.

"No thanks, mom. I think I'll hang out here." Jason felt dread. He recalled this day all too well. He felt shame at what he was about to do once she left.

"Are you positive, sweetheart? It might be entertaining. Grandpa let me use his pickup. I'll buy you a soda pop. What do you say? Like old times?" She reached over and brushed young Jason's hair from his eyes with her milky white hand.

From the window, Jason reached up at the same time and touched his forehead. For a moment, it seemed as if he could feel his mother's gentle, icy hand caress over his head. His spirit shattered as he watched her walk towards the door. He hoped she would walk through the door to the other side, where he stood. She vanished instead. With dread, Jason turned back to his younger self and observed him dashing to the window. He peered through his older self as he waited for his mother to drive out of sight to the store. Young Jason turned back and grabbed the cigarettes his mother had left behind on the table. Jason watched his younger self slide out the first of many cigarettes to come from the pack. His heart fell as young Jason lit the end and took a sharp draw. His face turned a strange shade of green before he ran to the bathroom.

Jason's soul dropped as all came clear. He spun around to the awaiting dog. "That was the first time I reached for you, wasn't it? I puked all night. My mother assumed I had caught the flu. She watched over me all night. She sat on the corner of my bed, placing a cold cloth to my head."

Fear tore through him as the dog sat up and growled again. Jason kept talking anyway. "You took my mother from me." Jason's hand shook as he felt that old, familiar bulge in his pocket. Reaching down, he yanked out his pack of cigarettes. Jason kept his eyes level with the dog's threatening glare. He held them up in front of the dog. "For years, you followed me. I have struggled to rid myself of you, but you came back." Jason crumbled up the cigarettes and threw the pack at the dog. "You can have them. I don't want them anymore." The dog growled louder. Jason stood firm with his bat in his hand, bracing to fight, but the dog became silent. His heart dropped as he watched the dog turn and glance into the woods.

Jason stared with disgust as another dog appeared, and this one was nastier than the last. He was enormous. The creatures' skin was stretched to its limits. What should have been healthy brown skin was a transparent tan instead. Its face was swollen, and its stomach was bloated. It had the same color eyes as the last dog, and they were embedded deep into the eye sockets. It tried to expose its teeth, but that seemed to be too much of a workout.

By the time the dog arrived at the porch, a low rumbling growl could be heard. Before Jason could speak to the dog, it vomited. Massive waves of thick, gold-colored puke spewed from his mouth. Jason suppressed a gag as the smell reached him. It stank like rotten yeast and stomach acid. Jason grabbed his shirt collar and lifted it up to his nose to block out the putrid odor.

When the dog finished, it licked its lips and turned to walk towards the woods. Jason realized he was expected to accompany him, and he didn't want to. He knew what this dog was, and he didn't wish to confront it. The dog, composed of ash, produced a warning bark as if to say, "Move or I'll attack". Jason stepped down from his mother's porch and side stepped the giant puddle of puke.

Jason followed the tan dog into the woods. This dog took a familiar path up the mountainside that Jason knew well. It was the route he and his friends walked and camped on. You name it, it happened there. Jason followed at a safe distance. It surprised him to see the glow of a bonfire in the distance. He could hear loud music and laughing. Jason realized he was headed to his old campsite. It felt wonderful to look at some of his former buddies sitting beside his seventeen-year-old self. Jason stood beside the second dog and studied the spectacle in front of him.

"Wow, that's Arnold over there, and that's Steve. I can't believe how young we all look. That's Abigail…" Jason's voice trailed off. "Look at her… still devastatingly beautiful." Jason watched as Abigail walked toward his teenaged self with her blonde curls bouncing up and down on her back. Abigail perched in his lap and played with his hair as she observed him talking to his friends. "Look at me. Stupid jerk! Look at her! She's crazy about you! You were lucky she married your stupid ass!" Jason's voice stumbled on dead air. "She had my children. With each child she bore for me, the light left her eyes. She figured out that I was nothing but a drunk. She deserved so much better... better than me. Abigail stayed longer than I deserved."

Jason scanned the landscape in front of him as he addressed the dog. "That's the night I met you. Damn... I felt so grown up the first time you touched my lips. I thought I had it all. I had the girl, the friends, and I had a promising education going for myself. But I welcomed you into my life and I never once questioned you. Why? Why did you come after me? I was somebody then. I was happy." A hot tear traveled down Jason's face as he continued to observe his adolescent self, put one beer after another to his mouth, and drink. "Arnold over there... you took him in that car accident. Steve didn't meet you until after his wife died five years ago. Everybody keeps urging him to accept help, but you won't let him, will you?" Jason said as he rubbed his face on the back of his sleeve. He stared at Abigail. "I lost her for good and my babies. When she moved out..." Jason shook his head as he watched the scene dissolving into the dark.

The hair on the back of his neck stood on end, and the two dogs on either side of him turned to look behind him. Jason felt the essence of pure evil as he rounded to deal with another dog.

This one, however, was pitch-black and its eyes were blood red. Its steps were bitter, measured, and it had a fiendish purpose. This dog was bigger than the first two. When it panted, it offered the misleading understanding that it was smiling and that made Jason's skin crawl. After it reached Jason, it did something unforeseen. It rose on its hind legs. Standing at its full height, the dog towered over Jason.

Jason took a step backward and glanced up into the crimson eyes, staring down at him. He started as the creature spoke to him in a rich baritone voice.

"My name is Atticus. Please do not be frightened." He said, with his heavy voice resounding through his breast.

"I know who you are. You are no friend of mine. You are a deceiver." Jason said timid.

"Now, Jason, don't be so unpleasant. Was it not I that supported you when your mother died? Where were your family or your friends? I was there for you when no one called to check on you. I was there when they neglected to show up at your mother's burial. Wasn't it I that took your hand when Arnold died? I have never let you down the way others have. I am your devoted companion." He replied with a deceptive sweetness in his tone.

"Yes, you were there. Not the way you make it out to be. I reached out to you because I was lonely. Not because you were my friend. I needed the suffering to go away and…"

"That's right, Jason. I removed that suffering, didn't I?" He added as he placed his heavy massive paw on Jason's shoulder. "I'm the one that never let you down. I numbed your misery and discomfort. I encouraged you to not give a damn."

Jason jerked his shoulder out from under the weight of the black dog's paw. "You took Arnold from me. You took my mother from me. How is that being my friend? When I had no money, you were nowhere to be found. You ditched me! I suffered all night, and I ended up selling everything I held dear. My mother's wedding ring I... I sold it for you. You let me down." Jason stepped away from Atticus. "You are a con artist! You did nothing but leave me desperate and destitute!" Jason felt his blood rush from his head as his words washed over the dog towering over him.

The ground shook as Atticus dropped on all fours and crouched as if to strike. Jason mustered up his courage and grabbed hold of his bat in both hands. "You terrify me. We both realize it. But you know what? You may have wrecked my existence until now, but you..." He said as he pointed his bat at the ashy dog. "And you..." He added as he lifted the bat to the bloated dog. "You have no power over me!"

The two dogs yelped as if someone kicked them as hard as they could. They ran and shielded themselves behind their master. "And you..." He said as he pointed the bat at Atticus. "You can try to slaughter me, but I swear on my life, I will execute you before you kill me! You profess to be people's friend, but you are destruction in disguise. Go back to hell where you came from! I am in control of me, not you!" Jason felt courage with each phrase that spilled from his mouth. He straightened his back, and he clutched his bat as he stood by for Atticus to charge.

Atticus growled as he bowed at Jason's feet. The other two dogs followed his lead. Jason smirked to himself as he watched them vanish into the obscurity until he no longer noticed their presence.

Jason closed his eyes. He felt light as air. His feet raised from the ground. He opened his eyes as the brisk wind flowed over his face.

Gently, he was carried to his mobile home. He touched down smoothly on his feet onto the porch. It seemed as if this extraordinary manifestation took place over a few days, but somehow it took place in one night.

Jason laughed as the sunlight grew and warmed his face. For the first time, he felt like he had a chance, like maybe there was hope for him. Thoughts of Abigail and their children passed through his mind. Getting sober didn't seem so dreadful after all.

Was Atticus real?

You live in the real world... what do you think?

Cove Creek

The sunlight beat down on Renee's back. The heat felt great on her tired muscles. October had arrived. The fierce cold followed close behind. It was nice to have some warmth on her skin. The pleasant day made her hungry for her favorite food truck in town. The Redheaded Hippie had the best burgers and seafood meals around. Renee could never pass it up when she came to visit the tiny town of Bryson. She wasn't the only one in need of a burger and sunshine. The Redheaded Hippie was hopping with customers. It was a popular food truck that parked on the street in front of the town's only taproom. The Dumbbell taproom was more than a place to have a beer. It was one of those homespun locations where the locals flocked together to talk and eat at the picnic tables placed outside for the patrons. They strung white fairy lights from the trees above the tables, and music blast from a pair of speakers mounted above their door. The atmosphere made Renee feel as if she were on vacation instead of on her lunch break.

Renee took in her surroundings as she waited for Eric to pick up their orders of burgers and fries. The rumble in her stomach was making the waiting harder by the minute. Fatigue plagued her body and rest was nowhere in sight. Renee and Eric had been at Sandy's house yesterday, all night, and most of the morning. It was the tenth time they had been to her residence in the past month. Renee thought Sandy was ridiculous, but that was her life as a Ghost Hunter.

Business had been disastrous since the economy went down in the toilet. Renee guessed everyone was willing to put up with the peculiar occurrences in their homes to save a dollar. No one had the extra cash to spend. Renee's mother kept advising her to get an actual job, but she couldn't let it go. The possibility that something was out there kept her going. She had witnessed strange things her entire life. After speaking to others about her experiences, she knew there had to be something to it.

"Lost again in deep thought, are we?" Eric said as he slipped onto the picnic table bench beside Renee. He arranged the food on the table as he awaited a response.

"Yeah, it's just one of those days, I suppose." Renee replied, as she unwrapped her burger.

"Renee, you realize this is just part of our profession. We investigate everything. We'll get a hit someday. Soon, I promise." Eric smiled the boyish grin Renee loved so much as he nudged her in the ribs with his elbow.

"I know. I just keep thinking about what my mom suggested. Maybe we should hang it up. We haven't had a decent reading in at least a year. Our equipment is ancient compared to what other people are using. We can't afford the new technology. We can scarcely pay our rent, let alone more machinery." Renee sighed as she poked her burger with her finger.

"First, your mom is wrong. Her opinion is old fashioned. Never listen to advice that would lead you anywhere other than the path that your dreams are on. You 're great at what you do, Renee. You'll prove it one day. I just know it." And with that sentiment, he took a gigantic bite of his burger and smirked. Renee couldn't help but feel faith in his reassuring words. Her hunger returned, and she put her burger back together and took a bite.

As she nibbled her burger, Renee listened to the discussions floating around the taproom picnic area. The word "Ghost" grabbed her attention. She turned her head toward two women sitting at a nearby picnic table. They sipped on bottled beer as they spoke in whispered tones.

"Yeah, I know. It was weird for that to happen again. I've said it a million times, don't go to death beach. I mean, people die there." One woman declared as she flipped her brown, glossy hair over her shoulder.

"I have to admit it, two deaths in one month are a little strange." The blond-haired young woman with the ponytail said as she clutched her beer in her hand.

Renee couldn't resist. She had to ask. "Excuse me?" Both women's heads snapped in Renee's direction with puzzled expressions on their faces.

"Yeah?" the brown-haired woman responded.

"I'm sorry; I didn't mean to overhear your conversation. What beach are you talking about? I wasn't aware there was a beach in this part of North Carolina." The two women glanced at each other and back to Renee. It was as if they were deciding on whether to tell her about the beach.

The blond answered this time. "There isn't a beach; it's a creek the residents and tourist go to. They call it the beach because it has a lot of sand. The sand extends from the creek bed into the grass where everyone lays out in the sun."

"Oh, why are you calling it death beach?"

"Well, tons of individuals die there every year. Not just drowning, but mysterious deaths. I have known people to collapse with heart attacks instantly after their feet contact the water. There are children who have drowned in an inch of water. They say it's haunted."

"Really? Has anyone seen a ghost?"

"Hey, you two are those ghost hunters that were in the newspaper a while back, aren't you?" The blond said with a sneer.

"Yes, we are that couple." Renee said, with a hint of irritation. Locals had taunted them too many times.

"I meant no offence; I think you two will be perfect to go there and check things out. It's just down the road, you can follow the signs." She replied as she pointed in the direction they needed to go. Renee could see she had worn out her welcome when the women turned their backs to the conversation.

Renee turned to Eric. "Let's go check it out. Maybe it could be our last hurrah." She added sarcastically. Eric rolled his eyes and gave a nod as he rose to tidy up his trash. Renee followed his lead before accompanying him to the car.

Eric headed down the street in the direction the women had pointed out. It was a well-known mountain road. Tourist traveled it regularly to swim, not knowing the grim history of the scenic route. There was a parking lot close to the beach area. It was packed full of vehicles. Eric was lucky to locate a parking space when a car backed out as he turned into the lot. They climbed out of the car and followed the sign that read, "Cove Creek."

Eric and Renee walked a few feet to a clearing that resembled a beach. The township had poured white sand close to the water. Inside the body of water there was a rope with a warning sign that read, "Swim at your own risk past this point."

They had a lifeguard chair, but no lifeguard on duty. There were children playing on it. Renee figured the town must have run out of funds to pay for a lifeguard. Maybe no one wanted the job because of the history of the beach. Looking around, Renee's initial impressions of the beach were not of ghosts and suffering. It was a serene sight to witness the families having barbecues and the children splashing in the water. There was nothing unusual about Cove Creek, at least during the daytime. With all the individuals there, Renee did not wish to make herself conspicuous with the ghost detection apparatus. "Let's come back tonight, around midnight." Renee said as she made her way back to the car.

When they reached home, they immediately unloaded the equipment from the night before. Sandy had plenty of outlets to plug in their machinery. Cove Creek, however, would not. They would have to rely on batteries. Eric placed the equipment they needed into the chargers. As Eric prepared the bags for the ghost hunt, Renee went upstairs to her room. After a much-needed shower, Renee set a clock alarm and took a nap.

When the alarm went off, Renee looked around her room. It was dark, and she was alone. Eric had been awake for a while. She could hear him moving around the kitchen. Renee knew this investigation would strike a nerve with Eric. His brother had drowned when they were children. Eric was hellbent on confirming, not only to the world, but to himself, there was life after death. In doing so, he would prove his brother was out there. Eric thought it was his fault his brother drowned. He had taken his little brother fishing. Eric knew his little brother couldn't swim. He had forgotten

B. D. West

the lifejacket that his brother always wore. Eric caught a fish and Timmy tried to scoop it up with a net. Timmy fell into the frigid water. Eric's mother told Renee that Eric almost drowned searching for his brother. It was clear to see why Eric needed to discover validation of life after death.

For Renee, the reason was simple. She thought she had seen a phantom in her grandmother's house as a teenager. Everyone called her a phony. Renee vowed she would prove it someday. She dragged herself out of bed, got dressed, and headed downstairs.

Eric was filling up bags and gulping coffee. "It's about time you woke up." He stated as he squeezed more equipment into a backpack.

"I'm raring to go. Let's blow this popsicle stand!" Renee replied as she headed out the door. She snatched a pouch of sweetgrass as she smacked Eric's backside on the way out. Eric grinned as he grabbed the bags and followed her out the door.

The mountain road, once immersed in sunshine, had taken on a foreign appearance. The moon was full in the night sky, casting its eerie light through the forests surrounding the road. After pulling into the empty parking lot, Eric and Renee immediately removed their sensory equipment from the vehicle. Renee reached into the car and grabbed the pouch of sweetgrass. When the grass was lit, it served as a natural repellent to angry entities. They had run into angry spirits before, and it wasn't pretty.

Setting their bags a few feet away from the water, they started the set up. First, Renee set up the infrared night vision video camera. It had a movement sensor that would activate the camera if anything moved.

Eric retrieved a thermocouple. The thermocouple was a gadget that helped him to identify hot and cold spots. He also brought out a digital tape recorder from his backpack to record EVPs. Electrical Voice Phenomena could be complex. An individual could pick up something real; however, some people question everything they can't see. There were plenty of skeptics in the world. Eric and Renee needed further evidence. Capturing pictures was a vital goal they shared.

Renee made a broad circle with the sweetgrass. She lit the ends until they smoked. The intense smell reminded Renee of how the lawn smelled after it had been cut. It produced a distorted sense of security at night.

After Eric and Renee were finished, they sat down on a blanket Renee had spread out on the grass in the protective circle. Renee checked her wristwatch. Five minutes until midnight. The hairs on the back of her neck stood up in anticipation. This time felt different. Renee could see Eric could sense it, too. The silence was deafening without the sounds of frogs chirping, owls hooting, or the crickets' songs filling the air. It was an odd phenomenon that would be hard to explain.

Just when Renee was about to check her watch again, the light turned on the video camera. Becoming alert, Renee tried to see through the darkness. She couldn't see anything. Eric stood up to investigate the camera. He peered into the viewfinder. "Everything is functioning... wait... what's that?" Eric glanced up toward the creek.

"What? What do you see?" Renee asked as she stood to her feet. She tried looking in the same direction as Eric.

Eric stared into the camera. "It's over the water; look!" He whispered as he stepped aside, mindful to not walk out of the protective circle. Renee looked into the camera. A vast blue light was swirling above the water. It looked like a maelstrom, but it sat upright, like a gate. It pulsed like an open neon sign in a storefront window. Before they could pull themselves away from the extraordinary sight, people wandered out of the whirlpool. Women, men, and children exited the blue light with somber expressions.

Renee looked up from the viewfinder. She didn't require the camera to view the supernatural people. They were wearing a translucent blue color around their bodies. The children caught Renee's attention. One child was a little boy; he appeared to be around the age of ten. He shuffled around crying as he inspected every tree and bush. The boy ran to the other ghost. He begged them to tell him where his parents were. Renee's heartbeat fast as the boy's milky blue eyes connected with hers. He raced towards Renee. The boy halted in front of the sweetgrass. "Do you recognize me?" The boy asked with a watery frown.

Renee glanced at Eric, then back to the boy. "No, I don't. I'm sorry; what's your name?"

"Thomas; can you help me locate my parents?" He pleaded with hope on his transparent face.

Before Renee could respond, the ghost drifted away. Renee watched him until her heart could take it no longer. She let her eyes wander around to the other ghost. There was a female in a bathing suit; she spread out a towel. She then drew out sunblock and smeared it all over her body. The sunbathing beauty lay down on her towel, as if the sunlight was shining over her icy frame.

In the distance, a little schoolgirl was skipping rope beside the creek as a man stood by with a fly-fishing rod.

Eric pointed to the lifeguard in the chair that had been vacant earlier that day as Renee looked on with fascination. If they didn't already know it was midnight, they would have thought Cove Creek was experiencing a summer's day. The ghost made the beach look alive with activities, picnics and sunbathers. Renee looked over at Eric, who was filming the remarkable event. He beamed to himself. He finally had the confirmation he desired. Renee watched with astonishment.

Snapping out of her wonderment, Renee's body jerked as a powerful, impassioned voice thundered from across the water. Pulsing red, the ghost headed straight for Renee and Eric. The closer the phantom came, the louder he sounded. The scary apparition looked like he had been at least fifty when he died, and he wore khaki shorts and a Hawaiian shirt. Advancing closer, the ghost walked up to the protective circle.

Renee jumped as the ghost yelled at her. "Who the hell are you? You're just here to make fun of us! Leave! You're not welcome here!" He stated as he landed a few punches into the defensive barrier the sweetgrass provided. The barrier vibrated. The lack of contact caused the man to become enraged.

"Please, sir… we are here to observe. Please settle down!" Renee yelled back. The irate man's shrill voice became stronger, making it impossible for Renee to hear the words leaving her mouth. She glanced over at Eric, and he was frozen with fear. Renee peeked around the irritable man. The other ghost had gathered in a tight group and looked on with dread. Renee could see they feared the hostile man. She glanced back at the ghost, and he was glaring at her with heavy contempt.

The ghost's eyes pulsed red. "You cannot have them. They are mine." He hissed.

Before Renee could deal with the man, he let out a savage growl. It was a deep, frightening noise. The growl sounded like a deranged dog. The ghost foamed at the mouth. Renee's fear intensified as the ghost changed from a transparent entity to a solid form. "This is not a specter," Eric whispered.

After punching the barrier over and over, he raised his fist in the air in a taunting way, as if he was impersonating a slow knock on a door. Drool dripped down his chin as he panted and scratched at the boundary. Renee searched her brain for anything she may have picked up or read that would provide an inkling of what to do next. Her mind turned up blank. She searched for her pouch. Maybe there would be something in there.

No such luck.

Renee looked up and inspiration struck her as the barrier collapsed. The man's foot crossed over the protective threshold. Eric abandoned his position at the camcorder and jumped on the demonic entity. Renee grabbed a fist full of blazing hot sweetgrass. She rushed up to the man and grabbed ahold of his face. With a violent thrust, Renee shoved the sweetgrass into his mouth. He tried to shriek, but the sweetgrass blocked his air-pipe. The entity clawed at his face as smoke spewed from his mouth, and he fell to the ground. Eric and Renee jumped back as they watched the entity thrash around until it became still. His body sank deep into the soil.

Eric and Renee stared at the spot as if they expected him to come back. Renee tore her eyes away from the ghastly sight. She looked at Eric as he, too, turned away from the grave and smirked at her. Eric thrust his arms around Renee's shoulders and laughed.

As they embraced and giggled, a thought crossed Renee's mind. Dread rippled through her as she remembered they were standing outside the protection circle. She pulled away from Eric and glanced around.

The group of ghosts left behind had surrounded them. They stared with various expressions of shock and disbelief. An elderly lady zigzagged her way through the group of ghostly souls. She found her way to the front. "You have released us; thank you." She replied with a smile.

Eric and Renee observed in silence as the ghost turned away. They returned to the maelstrom on the creek and disappeared.

A realization settled over Renee. "We can't show the footage. These souls had been people at one time. That devil held them as hostages here."

Eric nodded his head. "Somehow it feels like it would be a betrayal to their memory."

Renee grinned. "I guess we leave here empty-handed once again."

Shaking his head, Eric replied. "Not really; I know my brother is out there. I'm going to find him."

Renee reached out and grasped Eric's hand. "You mean, we are going to find him." Together they would locate Eric's brother, and the trapped spirits that could not move on.

Their ghost hunting days had only begun.

Lights out

Ava drummed her fingernails on the counter at the dry cleaners where she had worked for two years. She hated being there, but she needed the job. Ava wished she could have gone to college like her friends the year after they graduated high school. Unlike their parents, Ava's parents were not wealthy. Her parents were blue-collar laborers. Each of them worked in a factory. Her dad made dashboards for diesel trucks and her mother made baby clothes. They barely had enough to pay the bills. Saving for college just wasn't in the budget. Ava's grades didn't qualify for a scholarship. Working for her Aunt Sue's dry cleaner was her only option. Most teens in Ava's town lived in dorms or at home with their parents and drove to school every day. She was proud that she could manage something they couldn't.

It was a Friday night. Ava didn't have any special plans. "Plump girls like me don't have many dates on Fridays. Tonight, I'll go to the grocery store. No date means a taco dinner kit, a movie and home to relax," Ava thought to herself as she looked up at the clock. "Yes!" it was five o'clock.

Ava went to her Aunt Sue's office. "Aunt Sue, I'm leaving." She announced with a grin.

Aunt Sue glanced at her wristwatch. "Is it five already? Gosh, where did the day go? Well, don't forget to clock out, sweetheart. See you Monday."

Running to the back, Ava grabbed her pocketbook and keys. She then headed to the front door. When she approached the door, she spun the closed sign around and locked the door. Ava walked across the street to her dented mustang. She adored that car. Most of the teens in town had brand new cars. Ava didn't care. She wouldn't trade her car for anything. It had character. The dull blue leather seats matched the cracked enamel of the car. Ava loved the way the engine cackled when she turned the key over. The hole in her muffler caused people to give her nasty looks. It was deafening. "They don't pay my bills. Why should I care?" Ava thought with a sneer. She pulled away from the curb and headed for the Brown-Bag-It grocery store. It was the biggest store in town. When the Brown-Bag-It moved into town, there was a lot of controversy. It put several small stores out of business; they couldn't compete with the store that sold everything you could imagine.

As Ava drove down the quiet street, she noticed clouds rolling in. She knew then she should hurry. Pulling into the parking lot, Ava found a spot close to the front entrance. "At least I wouldn't get too wet if it rained." Ava mumbled to herself as she climbed out of her automobile.

The doors of the store slid open, and a rush of frosty air blew into her face. It felt wonderful. It became humid in the mountains before it rained. Ava didn't have an air conditioner in her car, and the humidity made her miserable. Welcoming the invigorating blast of the Brown-Bag-It air conditioning, Ava wandered over to the metal rack and seized a small shopping cart. As Ava headed toward the first aisle, a greeter spoke. "Hello and welcome to Brown-Bag-It grocery store. If there is anything I can do to make your shopping experience better, please let me know." Ava didn't acknowledge her. She had heard that line many times. Most people didn't take notice. It didn't upset the door greeter. Ava heard her start the same sentence to someone behind her as she pushed on through.

Lettuce was first on her list. Ava loved to pile on the lettuce and cheese on her tacos. "Maybe that's why there is a little extra on my rear," Ava scalded herself as she navigated through the colorful vegetables.

Ava picked out the freshest head of lettuce they had. Next, she moved up and down the aisles to pick up the taco dinner kit, cheese, and sour cream. Her mouth watered and her stomach rumbled.

After grabbing a soda, Ava headed for the checkout line. The front of the store had enormous picture windows. Ava could see it had become dark outside. The storm clouds had blotted out the sunlight. It was capturing the attention of the patrons waiting to be checked out. The sky was pitch black and rolling with thunder and lightning. Before Ava knew what was happening, a roll of thunder hit. It rang out like a sonic boom. Then several events took place at once. The electricity blinked twice, and it suddenly went black. A wave of "oohs" and a few "oh no's" ripped through the store. The rain poured with an intense purpose. Ava was merely speculating, but it sounded like a twister was blowing over.

The faculty of the grocery store jumped into action. They acted like soldiers on a military base. Everyone knew what to do and where to be. The managers handed out flashlights and barked orders. The staff moved fast. One manager called out. "Everybody in the store, make your way to the front, please! Everyone in the store please make your way to the front."

While everyone's attention was pulled towards the front of the store. Ava turned around and watched the store's militant staff move in the back of the store. Flashlights were traveling up and down the aisles as the workers searched for stragglers or potential thieves. Ava hated to admit it to herself, but the managers made her feel uneasy. She had never been in a store when the power had gone out. She was unclear of how to respond. Ava looked around at the concerned faces observing as two beefy looking stock boys moved to the front doors. The managers were repeating, "They can leave, but no one can enter!" No one was leaving in the beginning. Some shoppers believed that the power would turn on. The rest didn't wish to go out there into the storm, including Ava. Some shoppers made small talk to lessen the tension. There were a few shoppers sitting on the benches that were by the front doors. Ava's feet ached after thirty minutes of standing in one place while she waited. One by one, Ava watched as people were abandoning their carts. Ava tried to keep the hope flowing. She didn't have any food at her house.

Another flash lit up the parking lot. This time it appeared from the road. It looked like a power line exploding in a luminous blue light. Ava looked around; she noticed the bag boys were removing bags from the ice machine into a cart. They took them to the meat department to save the store's merchandise. Other workers methodically collected the abandoned carts loaded with food. They promptly returned the items to the shelves. Ava had no idea the store was so efficient.

The storm became worse. Ava had never witnessed a thunderstorm of that magnitude before. Before she knew it, the manager yelled out, "For everybody's safety, no one is to leave the store! There is a substantial threat out there!"

The beefy stock boys moved to the middle of the door way. Ava felt anxious. They looked as if they were ready to hurt someone if they were confronted.

Ava abandoned her cart and proceeded to the front window. She peered out into the storm and prayed for it to end. The rain poured down with heavy sheets spraying the windows. Ava couldn't see two feet in front of the store.

"It's strange they have to keep people here for their safety. I wonder why people go out in that kind of weather," Ava thought to herself as she watched the raindrops hit the glass.

"I love a good storm." A man stated as he stood with his back to the window.

Ava jumped at the strong tone in his voice. It pierced through the heavy tension like a knife. Looking over at him, Ava couldn't help but appreciate the man was handsome. He had shoulder-length blond hair. It was drawn at the nape of his neck. He appeared as if he were relaxing in the sun in the park. He had a serene demeanor that looked unusual for someone riding out a vicious storm. The deep blue pinstriped suit he wore made his sharp blue eyes stand out. Ava didn't know how to respond to him. She shifted back to the window and ignored him. It was the greeter from the front of the store who spoke to him.

"I can't agree with you, sir. I mean, that is a scary storm out there, not to mention dangerous." She replied as she plucked out a hair tie from her pocket and yanked her hair into a bun.

"I don't mean to sound blasé. I am a professional observer, so to speak. I enjoy observing reactions to storms. Fascinating." He answered with a half grin.

Ava rolled her eyes. She recognized he was baiting the consumers, but she bit, anyway. "What could be so appealing about people's reactions?" She responded in disbelief.

"Ah, I see you don't appreciate my opinion. That is okay. I'll clarify. I learn a lot about myself and human nature. It helps me with my approach to individuals. I can read people because of it. For instance, I can see that you're a homebody. This isn't your first visit to the store this week. I sense deep loneliness from you. I can sense you want out of this godforsaken town, but you lack the necessary funds. You have a lot of suppressed passion inside of you." He replied as he peered into Ava's eyes. Her heart raced. She wanted to yell at him for his arrogance. He embarrassed her in front of other people, and her reaction slowed. Before Ava could counter, he threw up his hands in false submission. "I'm sorry; I should not have done that. It's a vulgar habit of mine."

"I thought it was cool! Do me!" The door greeter exclaimed with excitement.

"Hum, you're a young woman with an abundance of spirit and determination. You have a knack for catching the guy you set your sights on. It is a clever trick, however, because you are not straight." He replied as he leaned toward her. He gave her a wink as her smile slipped off her face.

"You're mistaken." She responded as she glared at him and turned her back. Everyone in the store became silent. It was the human reaction to having a strange person in your presence. No one knows what to do, so they try to avoid the individual until they leave.

The shoppers shifted from one foot to the other as they became tired of standing. Ava looked at her wristwatch, seven o'clock. She had been there two hours, and the rainfall had not let up. The air-conditioned store was becoming stagnant and hot. The bodies of the shoppers packed together formed a heat wave.

Ava looked around. The flashlights were still drifting around the store. There was no one trying to shop. It was for the security of the store. Anyone that had been shopping before was now up front near the windows. It was too dark to sit anywhere else. Ava counted ten shoppers. The rest were employees.

Hail beat against the windows. Ava turned her back to the storm and slipped down the wall. She sat down on the cold floor as she arranged her pocketbook in her lap.

"It must be tough being lonely." The man in the suit said as he focused in on Ava.

"Sir, if you don't mind. I don't care to talk to you." Ava replied with as much patience as she could muster up. Her mom repeatedly instructed her to not make crazy people angry.

"Yeah, man, why don't you leave her alone? We are just trying to ride out this storm. Unfortunately; we have to do it here in the store." Said the beefy stock boy by the door. Ava looked up at him and smiled.

The manager moved to the front with a small cart loaded with cold drinks. She handed them out to everyone. "I realize it's stifling in here, guys. Hang in there. This storm will be over before you know it. I have seen a million dreadful storms in my life. This one is rough too, but this too shall pass." The manager smiled at each of us as she passed out the refreshments. The curious man in the suit waved her away, however. He evaluated the manager as she shuffled past him.

"What a lovely name." He stated as he pointed to her nametag. "Victoria, I always thought that name sounded like refinement in its simplest form." He grinned at Victoria as she gawked at him. "You have a desire for beauty, don't you? I'd wager you were told your entire life how ugly you were. You became consumed with making yourself beautiful. From the scars behind your ears, I can see you have had some work done. That doctor of yours is a miracle worker, yes?" He added with a mischievous grin.

Victoria stood frozen. Her bottle of soda hit the floor. Thunder slammed against the blackened clouds. "Just who the hell do you think you are?" She replied in an unsteady tone.

The beefy stock boy moved away from the door he was guarding and stood near his boss. "Look, like I explained to you just a minute ago, leave the customers and my boss alone. If you can't be quiet, I'll be obliged to put you out. I know you don't want to go out in that storm, do you?" His chest heaved with restrained outrage.

"Tommy, is it?" The odd man replied as he scanned the stock boy's nametag. "I can read you too. How many breaks do you take to explore the porn websites on your employer's computer when she's not watching? You can do what you want, correct? Your mommy always says boys will be boys, right?" He added with a boyish grin that looked out of place on his face. The longer he remained there, the more Ava noticed his face changing. He appeared older, yet he didn't. It was almost as if he was hiding the wrinkles behind stage make up.

Tommy approached the man. "Look, I don't know who you have been speaking to. I think you need to check your facts before you run that fat mouth of yours." He replied as he cracked his knuckles in the man's face. The strange man chuckled. Everyone who had been making small talk had become silent to observe the spectacle unfolding.

The thunder became louder, and the lightning became brighter. "You're like sheep; easily led anywhere. Even to the slaughter. I can read you because I have been around a long… long time." He laughed harder.

"Take you for an example." He stated as he pointed to the woman sitting close to a young man with his arm around her. "You're not even supposed to be with him, are you? Where is your husband?" He giggled as he watched the woman's face turned red.

"And you, you're just pissed because you need a brew and wifey-poo won't let you. You're thinking about stepping back to the beer section and devouring one right now, aren't you?" The visitor said as he pointed to the man in hand-me-down clothes.

"And you are looking all distinguished in your business suit. I bet when you hired your employees, you failed to point out that you are on the sex offender's registry. You secretly wish you were still at it. I am confident your co-workers would be interested to see the pictures you keep in your glove box." He declared to the manager gawking at him with his mouth open.

"And you, miss lonely heart. I relate to you. I too walk this world alone and no one would notice if I disappeared from existence. You suffer from gluttony, unfortunately. Some people choose whiskey; you chose food to drown out the pain. You wished to go to college, didn't you? Did your parents give a damn about you? Did they save the cash you would require for college? Of course not, they ordered you to sink or swim and you sank." He said as he exposed his teeth. All of them were sharp and jagged. They poked his lips as he spoke. Small drops of blood pooled on his bottom lip. The thunder crashed down around the store. The rain changed to blood. It splashed crimson against the window. A quick round of gasps swept through the patrons as they backed up against the wall.

As he glanced around at the alarmed faces, his grin became deranged, and his eyes became blood red. Ava slid up the wall to stand on her feet. Fear ripped through her soul as he twisted to look at her. "You're brave… afraid… but brave."

"Who are you?" Ava whispered.

"I knew you would be the one to ask." He answered as his front tooth pierced his lip once again. Blood oozed down his chin. "I am obscurity."

"Are you the devil?" Ava said with ambivalence.

"I have many names. I prefer them all. They strike dread in all of you. You make me strong. You help me survive." He hissed like a serpent as he whispered.

Ava knew she had to stand up to him or die. "I'm not afraid of you!" She answered as powerful as she could. "Go away!"

He snickered with an unusual noise in his throat; it was deep, like a growl. "How dare you tell me what to do!

You're not enough to make me go away!" He spat again, this time producing a snake like tongue.

Ava looked around at everyone. "Come on! Stand up to him! He is feeding off of our fear!" She held out her hand. Ava felt grateful as one by one; everyone stood up to hold her hand. "We are not afraid of you! Go back hell to where you belong!" The intruder's face became contorted with resentment as he paced. He thrust his hands up in the air and shrieked. The noise was so intense the windows shattered.

A silvery light flashed, and a mighty charge hurled them backward. Ava lost her grip on Tommy's sweaty hand and smacked her head against the wall. A warm sensation dribbled down her neck. She placed her palm against her head and pulled herself into a sitting position.

The strange man had vanished, and so did the storm. The shoppers felt disoriented. Some were struggling to reclaim their balance, while others attended to the injuries of the customers.

Ava stood to her feet. She turned and glanced outside. The sun was setting, and the birds were chirping. It was as if nothing had transpired. There was no evidence on the ground that it had rained blood.

After the EMTs had checked on Ava, she went home. She watched the news to see if they would talk about the odd events or mention the devil. The reporter passed it off as a freak storm that had isolated itself over the grocery store. Ava, however, experienced something different. She knew she had looked at pure evil.

The devil appearing in a freak storm was something they would never report on the evening broadcast.

Night and Day

Sara sat at her makeshift vanity and brushed her hair with her mother's brush. Her vanity was just a folding table, and a cracked full-length mirror she had recovered by the side of the road. She draped a pink sheet over the table to give it a fancy flare. Sara arranged her perfume bottles and hair combs just the way she liked it. She only had three perfume bottles left. The monster broke the other ones. He smashed them because they were her mother's and he wanted to see her to cry. Her mother's hairbrush was the last memento she had left of her mother's existence. She had to lie to the monster. She told him she bought it at a yard sale so he wouldn't break it.

The hairbrush was the same as it had been when her mother used it to brush Sara's blonde hair. A pain shot through Sara's rib cage as she thought to herself, "What would mamma think if she saw my face and thin hair?" Sara stared at her battered face. Black and purple skin covered the left side of her milky white skin. The right side of her mouth was in the last stages of recovery from the last violent blow with its hints of green and yellow.

Sara struggled to recall the last time she wept. She practiced holding in the tears for the past three years since he broke her perfume bottles. It gave the monster what he wanted. He needed to see her slowly dying from the inside. The monster was dead inside, and the dead loved their company. Sara tried to seek help from the law enforcement.

They advised her to go to the Department of Social Services, make a citizen's arrest, or run to a relative's house. The D.S. S told her they could put her in an apartment, but it was only temporary. They said if a woman with children needed it, she would have to leave.

Making a citizen's arrest was a joke. How could they think that Sara, in her 5 foot 3 inches, could arrest him? The monster was 6 foot 3 inches and three hundred plus pounds. As far as relatives went, her mother was all she had left. She passed a year after Sara had married the devil. Sara's mother dying was the worst day of her life. The monster told her to suck it up. Where was Sara to run? She had no money and no realistic place to go.

The monster at least let her go for strolls in the evening. Well, at least Sara preferred to pretend he knew, and he was letting her have peace. In the real world, he was watching television while he drank himself in to unconsciousness. It had been an hour since she last heard him cuss at the television or stomp to the refrigerator for another beer.

Sara rose from her grey folding chair and walked to her bedroom doorway to take a peek. The monster was stretched out in his recliner with his feet dangling off the end. His beer bottle was lying on its side with left over beer spilling out onto the floor. Sara tiptoed past him and out the front door. She closed the door as softly as she could.

Next, she stood still to listen to hear if there was any movement behind the door. If she heard him stir, she would run to her bedroom window and crawl back into the house. Nothing moved, and she released the breath that she was holding.

Sara spun around and let the sunshine warm her skin. It felt wonderful to feel the freedom of the outdoors. She skipped off the porch and started her walk down her usual trail. She couldn't take the main road. People would stop and attempt to take her to the emergency room like they did a few months ago. Sara found it safer to wander through the woods. She didn't run into anybody in the woods. Sometimes, she could walk in the park; normally it was clear of people. When Sara got to the park's wooded edge, her spirit dipped. The Park was crowded with people. There were families and children running around, throwing footballs, baseballs and having cookouts. Sara remembered when the monster used to take her there. He would cook hamburgers on those iron park grills. He had a way of making her feel special. It was like she was the only person in his world that could make him happy. Sara's heart shattered as she thought of the way he used to grin at her.

Turning away, Sara drew a deep breath. She searched around the woods for one of the park's trails. Sara tried to visualize where the trailheads were. If she was correct, one would be not very far from where she was standing. With a new purpose, Sara walked again. The fall leaves were crunching under her feet as she stepped around the trees in her path. Her feet became fatigued. She had been hiking for over thirty minutes without locating the trail.

Sara paused and listened. She could hear children and people in the distance. Sara knew she couldn't have gone too far from the park. She glanced around to determine if she could see a trailhead marker. As she twisted in a circle to scan her surroundings, she saw it. Camouflaged by leaves and vines stood a house. How long it had been there, she couldn't guess. The home had been there for a long time. The peeling white and orange bricks looked strong enough to withstand time itself.

Two enormous trees stood on either side of the dwelling. The branches bent over the roof like they were protecting the tiny residence. The front porch was resting on the ground in a wooded heap. Nature had taken away its ability to be useful. The front door was painted a worn green.

Sara stepped up to the window on the right side of the door and peeked in. It was dark, but she could make out furniture and curtains. It was like someone got up one day, walked out, and never returned home. She moved to the door, stood on her tippytoes, and tested the knob. It surprised her to discover that it opened easily. Sara put her foot in the doorway and hoisted herself into the house.

If Sara didn't know what day it was, she would have sworn she stepped back in time. A breakfast nook with a white oval table and matching white chairs sat in the corner. A piano was pushed slightly away from the wall; browned sheet music rested on its top. A deep pink sofa and matching chair sat around an antique coffee table with a dusty guitar case sitting on top.

The floor had a Persian rug underneath the sofa and chair. The rug might be black if it hadn't been caked with grime. Under the soot, Sara could see what looked to be red and blue flowers braided into the background.

Sara closed her eyes and took in the quiet. No television playing a football game too loud, no cussing, and no beer belch echoing against the walls. Best of all, the beast wasn't there.

Sara checked her watch. She had been gone for over an hour. The fear of being gone too long passed over her. With regret, she turned around and left the mysterious house in the woods.

When she arrived home, Sara crept to the bedroom window and snuck in. She peeped around the doorway and felt relieved to see the monster was as she had left him. Sara tiptoed to the bathroom to wash her face and put on her nightgown. It was early, but dark outside. The thrill of finding the house in the woods had worn her out. She slipped between the cool sheets. As she drifted off to sleep, she thought of the next time she could sneak out and explore the little home.

It was two weeks before Sara could sneak out again. The monster had been on one of his paranoid streaks, and he watched her every move. He spoke to her as if she could leave him or cheat on him at any minute. The monster ended the charade, as expected, with brutality. It wasn't too bad; he just refreshed the bruise on her lip. "So much for the old ones getting any better," Sara thought to herself.

Same as last time, Sara waited until the beast passed out before she headed out the door. As soon as she was free of the monster's house, Sara broke into a run. She only had an hour before she was to return to the monster's lair. If she ran, she may have more time to spend in her little getaway.

Sara reached the house in record time. This time, she noticed the door was standing open. She wandered to the front door and peered inside. "Hello?" When no one responded, Sara climbed into the house once more. Everything was as she left it; except this time, she noticed a gramophone sitting on the white oval table. She glanced around the home once more to make sure she was alone. All was quiet. Sara walked up to the gramophone. A record was placed on the turntable. She reached out to the brass crank on the side of the player and twisted it a few times. Next, she released the metal latch, and the record began to spin. Excitement flooded her senses as she arranged the needle on the vinyl record.

A silky voice crooned to her from the wooden horn on top of the gramophone. The man with the dreamy voice sang of his heart falling for a woman the first night they met. He declared she tied a string around his heart, and he was sure it was love. Sara placed her hand over her heart and wished the powers that be could grant her a love like that. When the song finished, she picked up the needle and placed it on the record once more. The song played again, and this time Sara pretended the man was talking to her.

Sara turned in a slow circle as she drifted over to the piano. She sat on the piano bench and delicately traced the keys. She wished she knew how to play, but her mother never could afford lessons. Looking up from the keys, Sara noticed a picture. It was a black-and-white photograph of a man with a dapper-looking haircut. He was grinning at the camera like a movie star. Sara felt her heart skip a beat as she imagined he was looking at her. A smile touched her bruised lips.

"Well, hello there, handsome. I wish I knew your name. I hope you don't mind me being in your house." Sara giggled at the silliness of her comments. "I sure hope you don't mind if I come back. I'm positive you can see from the expression on my face, I'm thrilled to be here."

The smile melted from Sara's lips. She reached out and traced the stranger's picture with her fingertips. "I wish you were real. I lead a reclusive existence. Truth be told, if I stay with my monster, I may not survive much longer. He's going to kill me if someone doesn't save me. No one is going to deliver me." Pain pinched Sara's lip as she forced a smiled. "I'm glad I found you today. It has been nice talking to someone again." Sara glanced at her watch. "I better leave before the monster wakes up. Can I come back tomorrow?" The black-and-white photo silently gave its consent. "That settles it then. I'll see you tomorrow, handsome."

Sara kept true to her word, and she returned the next day. In fact, she came back every chance she could. When the beast passed out, Sara rushed to her home in the woods. Each time she returned; the dwelling would be altered. A fire would be lit in the fireplace, a different record would be on the gramophone turntable, and the black-and-white photograph would be moved.

The photo would sit on the table with tea for two or on the floor by the fireplace with a blanket. At first, the house scared her, but then the magic of the house lured her in. The winter months were coming quick. Sara found herself looking forward to the cheerful fires the home would have waiting for her.

It took her monster only two hours to drink himself into a stupor. Sara became giddy with excitement. Christmas was two days away, and she had bought her house a present. She couldn't wait to give it to the peaceful dwelling she considered her real home. She seized her wrapped package and slipped out the door. Fresh snow was falling to the ground. It made her journey to the house a magical one.

Surprise overtook her as she approached the house. The home had painted itself white and gave itself pink shutters on the windows. The steps had been rebuilt as well. Sara's home was complete. She held her present closer to her heart as she ascended the steps. The door opened for her before she could turn the doorknob.

The interior of the home was decorated for Christmas. A miniature Christmas tree sat on top of the white oval table next to the gramophone. Colorful paper chains, strings of popcorn, and cranberries hung from the branches. A cheerful fire popped and cracked in the fireplace as Christmas music played on the gramophone.

Sara looked around for the photograph that was always waiting for her. This time it lay on the floor in broken glass. Sara dropped her present onto the pink sofa and rushed to her picture. "Oh, no; what has happened to you, my love?"

Carefully taking the edge of the photo, Sara removed the picture from the glass. She looked at her photo tenderly as she dusted off the shattered glass. "You poor thing, I'll try to find you another frame."

Sara turned the photograph over to dust off the other side. "Hey... look at this. It's your name." Tears burned her eyes as she read his name aloud. "Your name is, Daniel." Sara turned the photo over to look at the man her heart belonged to. "Your name is, Daniel. Nice to meet you, Daniel."

The man in the photo seemed to smile brighter at Sara as she repeated his name over and over. "Well, Daniel, I brought you a gift." Sara rose to her feet and walked over to her pink sofa. She propped the photo up against a cushion. "I bet you are wondering, what in the world has this chick gone and bought me. Well… guess no longer." Sara unwrapped her gift and held it up to show Daniel. "It says home is where my heart is." Reaching out with her fingers, Sara touched the picture. "My heart is with you, Daniel."

Sara hummed to herself as she found a free nail on the wall and hung her photo. "Looks perfect, doesn't it?" She stood back and studied her handy work before shifting back to her photo. "I sure wish I could live here with you, Daniel." Sara glanced up from the photo and noticed two glasses of wine by the fireplace. The crystal glasses gleamed in the firelight. She picked up Daniel's photo and sat on the blanket by the fire.

As Sara sipped from her glass, she looked down at the hearth. A small black box was waiting for her. She placed her glass on the floor and propped Daniel against his wineglass. "Daniel, what have you gone and done?" Sara reached for the box and held it in both hands. The box was covered in black velvet. It felt like a miniature rabbit in the palm of her hands. She reached with her right hand and opened the box. Her breath caught in her throat. A blue sapphire ring cushioned in diamonds and gold sparkled in the firelight. "Oh, Daniel, I… I'm speechless. Are you asking me to stay with you?"

Sara removed the exquisite ring from its box and slipped it onto her finger. "I want to stay… I do. But…" Wiping the tears from her cheeks, she continued. "You know about the monster. He will kill me if I don't come back."

Before Sara could entertain the thought of leaving her husband, the monster's voice rang out. "Sara! I know you're in there! Get your ass out here!"

The blood drained from her face as Sara stood obediently to her feet. She walked over to the door and opened it. The monster's fist looked like boulders as he stood in the snow. "Yes, sir?"

"Don't you yes, sir me! Who the hell are you in there with?"

Shaking her head in disbelief, Sara spoke. "How did you find me?"

The monster rolled his bloodshot eyes. "You left tracks in the snow, dumbass! Answer me! Who's in there with you?"

Sara shook her head. "No one."

"I overheard you speaking to someone in there! Tell him to come out here and face me like a man!" The monster leaned his head to the side as he worked to see around Sara. "Come out and face me, you prick! You wife stealing, cow humping coward!"

"I told you, no one is here but me!" Sara broke her streak and sobbed. "I went for a walk, and I found this place. I was talking to myself."

The monster smirked. "Oh yeah, then who the hell is that?"

Sara followed the monster's thick, pointed finger. She jumped back as the man with the dapper smile stood beside of her. Her words came out in a whisper. "Daniel?"

Daniel winked at Sara before turning a vicious glance over at the creature in front of him. "I'm only going to say this to you one time, Mr. This is my fiancé, and you are trespassing. Remove yourself from my property at once or I will do it for you."

The monster raised his foot, teasing a step forward. "Oh, yeah? What are you going to do? You ain't nothing compared to me! I own her!"

Sara watched in horror as the monster took a step forward. She glanced over at Daniel, who was grinning from ear to ear. "Well… then I would do this." Daniel closed his baby blue eyes. The ground shook as the two trees on either side of the house lifted their massive roots from the earth. The tree on the left swung violently as it began its assault on the beast. The monster screamed as blow after deadly blow was delivered to his body. The tree on the right dug a hole with its mighty roots. When the hole was deep enough, the tree on the left wrapped a root around the monster and drug it kicking and screaming into the six-foot ditch. Both trees covered up the monster as it choked on its own blood and dirt before returning to guard the tiny home. The creature had been silenced.

Daniel opened his eyes. He looked over at Sara and grinned. "You said someone needed to save you. I'm here, my love."

Sara looked up into Daniels' eyes. "Are you real?"

"For you, I am."

Sara glanced over at the pile of dirt where the devil was buried. Snow was covering the evidence of his demise. Next to the monster's grave was an old headstone that read, "Our dear boy, Daniel, 1900-1929."

Smiling to herself, Sara realized she was free. Daniel had slain the beast.

Daniel reached out and grasped Sara's hand. He led her back into the house he had built just for her.

Sara belonged to him… she belonged to the house.

Johnny's Apple seeds

Mary Beth dug her wrinkled hands through the smooth black soil in her garden. After all, the best way to get rid of the weeds is to go on all fours and utilize the tools Mother Nature had provided her. It felt good; it was like she was a part of nature itself. She sat up on her knees, mopped her forehead with the clean side of her hand, and inspected her work. The tomatoes were fuller than last year, but the rabbits ate most of her cabbage. Overall, she was pleased with the fruits of her labor. If only the neighborhood children would be a little quieter, so she could enjoy her own backyard for once. How many times had their ball landed in her flowers? Too many to count, that's for certain.

As quickly as the thought left her mind, a loud commotion broke out in the neighbor's backyard. A familiar dark red ball sailed over Mary Beth's fence. Dead silence followed. Mary Beth smiled to herself as she strained to listen to the heated, whispered argument taking place between the petrified children.

They had given Mary Beth the title of the town witch. Why? She had never known the reason. Perhaps it was because she kept to herself. Maybe it was because she turned her lights off and left one candle burning in the window on Halloween night. She refused to come to the door to hand out candy. Sadness filled her soul, and the smile dropped from her face. "Stupid brats, what do they know anyway," she thought to herself. Mary Beth stood up and dusted off her knees and hands. She strolled over to her apple tree by the fence and picked up the ball. She turned to throw it over the fence when she noticed a young boy standing there with a terrified expression on his face. Mary Beth bounced the ball in her hand and narrowed her eyes. "I guess you lost the coin toss. Is this your ball, young man?" The boy started. He was not expecting her to speak to him, or maybe he hoped she wouldn't speak to him.

"What's the matter? Cat got your tongue?" Mary Beth replied as she arranged the ball between her arm and her hip. She tapped her foot. "It must have escaped your attention, but I'm an elderly woman living on borrowed time. Now, is this your ball or not?"

The boy swallowed and mustered up his courage. "Yes... it is. I would appreciate it if you gave it back." He held out his pudgy hands, trying to not let them tremble.

"Hum... why should I? After all, it seems to me this ball has broken over a quarter of my flowers I grew this spring. I should stick a knife right in the middle of it. I should put it out of its misery."

"You do that and I'll... I'll..." The boy's plump, sweat-streaked face struggled for words that wouldn't come.

"You'll do what?" Mary Beth replied as she watched the perspiration drop from the boy's blond hair and down his portly, rose-colored cheeks. She let him off the hook and tossed him the ball. "What's your name, kid?"

The young boy captured the ball with one big clumsy gesture. Satisfied he had a firm grip, he glanced up at Mary Beth. "Madison."

"Madison? What kind of name is that? That's not a people's name; it's the location of a town or road." Mary Beth responded with heavy sarcasm.

"It's the name my mom gave me." Madison shot back.

Mary Beth smirked and nodded her head. She recognized his kind all too well. These kids now days were nothing but smartasses. Too many unearned privileges, not enough discipline, and in most instances, there was a nonexistent parent. "You know, a smart mouthed kid would never have spoken to an elder like that when I was a child." Mary Beth crept closer to Madison and whispered, "Johnny Apple Seed would have come to claim you."

Walking around Madison's dumbfounded expression; Mary Beth strode over to her back porch. She hobbled up the three narrow steps to her favorite rocking chair. The sunset was bathing her old wooden rocking chair in splashes of orange and gold. The light made the porch look like a piece of heaven. Mary Beth sat down in the chair and rocked back and forth. She used her apron to fan herself from the fall heat. She closed her eyes and let the sunlight warm her fatigued, arthritic bones.

"Are you talking about the kid who planted all the apple trees?" Madison snapped.

Mary Beth's eyes shot open. She held up her wrinkled hand to shield her eyes from the sunlight. Taking in the young boy's expression, she retorted. "Is following old ladies around a new game for you? You could kill old people that way, you know." Mary Beth was pleased to see Madison's peaked curiosity. "Johnny was an inquisitive boy too, you realize."

"You are talking about Johnny Apple Seed? The boy who wandered across the country and planted the apple trees, right? I mean, that's what they tell us in school."

"Are they still circulating that lie?" Mary Beth chuckled.

"Well… what is the actual story?"

"You don't need to hear a story like that. It's a tremendous burden to know the truth. I mean, what are you, seven?"

"I want to hear it. I'm ten years old for your information. I know lots about responsibility. I take care of my baby brother when my mom goes to the store. I'm a lot more grown up than I look. I've kissed a girl and smoked a whole cigarette by myself. Trust me, I can be responsible." Madison responded with a cocky smirk.

Mary Beth laughed. "A whole cigarette, huh? You are practically a man already." Mary Beth said as she studied the young boy. "Being innocent happens only once. You don't want me to open that door and take that from you."

Madison crossed his arms in defiance. "Lady, do you watch the news or television? I can take it." he declared as he sat down on the porch step uninvited.

"I too was once an ignorant kid. I thought I knew it all. I was an only child and spoiled, much like you. I demanded a story every night from my father. When he became ill, my aunt came to live with us. She was a miserable old woman. I was determined she would take over for my father and weave me a tale like he would to put me to sleep. She told me the tale of Johnny Apple Seed. Don't let the stories that are told in school mislead you. In this story… the true story, no one lived happily ever after."

Mary Beth reached into her shirt pocket and removed a cigarette. Madison watched her close as she lit the tip end and inhaled. She blew out a large puff of smoke as she proceeded. "Let me tell you, kid. Cinderella never escaped the slavery forced on her by her stepmother after her father died. The mermaid committed suicide after she found out her human was in love with another woman. Snow White was executed in the dark woods. They stuffed her mangled body into a hollow tree while her stepmother placed herself on the throne. The history of Johnny Apple Seed was no different from the frosting covered versions of Hollywood." Taking another drag of her smoke, Mary Beth went on. "Once upon a time, parents used to tell the true story. Over time, huge production companies made everything clean and bearable for children. You kids are brats because you fear nothing."

Madison shook his head. "That's not true. We are afraid of a lot of things; just different things than you."

Mary Beth smirked. "You're a smart kid. Johnny was a sharp and inquisitive young man, too. I am unsure of the year this story took place. But I know that we have passed this story down in my family for generations."

Studying Madison's face one last time, Mary Beth went on. "Johnny's father was a farmer, and he was a widower. It's said that the sorrow from losing his wife would have consumed him had it not been for his son she left behind. He adored Johnny and spent every waking moment teaching him the trade of cultivating the land. Johnny's father wanted him to be a farmer some day and take over the family farm to continue his legacy. But Johnny rejected the idea. He wanted to board the ships to this place called America everybody was talking about. America was the land of limitless possibilities. He thought he could find places in America no one had discovered. Being a farmer and planting apple trees was out of the question. So, when Johnny turned fifteen, he left home. The image of his father's saddened expression as his father stood on the weather-beaten boat dock, burned deep into Johnny's soul."

Mary Beth took one last draw of her cigarette before flicking it into the yard. "As Johnny sailed away, he let the excitement of his adventure wash over him. He daydreamed of his new future waiting for him in America. England, in Johnny's mind, never existed. But isn't that just like a youngster? They Dream so big that the important details and loved ones are overlooked."

Madison scrunched up his face. "So, what happened next?"

"When he came ashore, he promptly discovered a colony that was eager to welcome him in. He found work as a blacksmith's apprentice. He hoped to work his way up to a full blacksmith someday. He adored his new way of life, and he wrote to his father to tell him about it. In his weekly letters, he sought to convince him to come to the new world to live with him. He wrote those letters faithfully until one day the last letter came back with a note from the undertaker. It explained that his father had died, and his father's farm had been sold to pay off some debt he had gained over the years. The letter further stated that his father's apple seeds were all he had to inherit. They included those seeds in the envelope."

Madison shook his head. "Well, that sucks ass. I bet he was hoping for money. Was Johnny sad?"

Mary Beth gave a serious nod as she responded. "Well, as you can imagine, despair set in. When the sorrow disappeared, anger came to stay. He was furious he had left his father behind. The rage became worse when he witnessed families around the village sharing happy times. Johnny carried his father's seeds in his pocket. Every day, he would reach his hand into his pocket to touch the seeds. He desired to once again feel his father's love, but it never came. The anger grew. Then one day, when Johnny reached into his pocket, he felt something peculiar. Pulling the seeds from his pocket, Johnny noticed a young sprout forming. He felt deep anguish. If the seeds were to die, it would be like losing his father all over again."

Fanning herself once more with her apron, Mary Beth went on. "Without thinking, he ran as quick as he could to the woodlands at the edge of town. He ran deep into the ancient woods where most men feared to go. Johnny came to a clearing and collapsed to his knees. He furiously dug with his bare hands through the roots and rocks. His fingernails cracked, bled, and ultimately tore loose from his fingers. Johnny dug into the earth until he was satisfied with his hole in the ground. He tenderly arranged the seeds into the ground, covered them up, and wailed bitterly. Tears soaked the turned-up soil. He sobbed until his body became weak with sorrow. He lay his head on the ground and fell asleep. When he woke up, a figure was standing over him."

Madison's eyes became wide. "Who was it?"

"It was something evil. The sinister figure told Johnny that his anger drew him there, and that he would collect him for his own. Johnny tried to fight, but in the end, he was not strong enough to resist the stranger. Meanwhile, the colonist noticed Johnny's absence. They suspected a wild animal had slaughtered him. That was, until the arduous winter set in. They claim it was the worst blizzard to strike since they had settled in that part of the mountains. Strange sightings of a pale young man standing at the edge of the woods circulated. Then, the children perished one by one under curious circumstances. The undertaker reported the children were white as snow and they had quarter sized holes all over their bodies. Worse yet, he said there was a strange worm in each hole with an arrow shaped head. It would peak out of the holes, and then it would go back in and devour the children's flesh from the inside out. They say that the smell was as if the child had been dead for weeks, yet it had only been hours." Mary Beth paused and smirked. "You're looking peaked, Madison. Maybe you are not as sophisticated as you claim you are. Maybe I should stop."

Madison swallowed a few times. "No, I can take it."

Mary Beth shrugged her shoulders. "Suit yourself. Anyway... where was I?"

"The kids were croaking." Madison chimed in.

"Right, well... no one knew what to make of this bizarre new plague that settled over their modest little town. What brought fear the most to the colonists was that the plague only touched the children. My ancestor, I think his name was Thomas, sat beside his son's bed every night. Thomas knew there was more to the strange deaths of the colonist children, and he was correct. One night, Thomas's fear came to life. He looked on with fright as Johnny invited himself into his son's bedroom. Johnny was as pale as a clean white linen sheet. His eyes were as silvery as winter's first snow. His pale blond hair draped over his eyebrow. Johnny walked soundlessly toward Thomas and his sleeping son. He reached into his tattered pocket and drew out seeds. The seeds were blood red, and they resembled miniature apples. They wiggled in his pale white hand, and they put out tiny, shrieks."

Mary Beth imitated the tiny scream before she proceeded. "Thomas watched Johnny approach his son. Thomas's son's skin split and peeled until quarter size holes appeared all over his body. The holes were pulsing as if they were standing by to welcome Johnny's seeds of death. In desperation, Thomas jumped in front of Johnny and yelled, take me, I'm old! I've lived my life. His life has hardly begun. Have mercy on my sleeping child! Johnny paused and studied Thomas. For a moment, he recalled the devotion his own father had for him. He stumbled backward, and the seeds spilled from his hand and hit the floor. The ground shook violently. Johnny fell back into the corridor and caught himself on the wall. He took one last look at Thomas with bloody tears rolling down his face. He turned, walked away, and disappeared into the night."

Raising her hands in front of her, Mary Beth's voice became dramatic. "Thomas scooped up his son as the ground shook below his feet. The house crumbled around him, and he barely made it out of the house alive. Thomas felt the bite of winter's night creep up his spine as he glanced towards the edge of the woods. He watched Johnny disappear into its vast darkness. Thomas then rounded to the ruins that were formerly his home and watched with melancholy as it became alight with fire. The fire was not like any flame he had seen before. The flames threw out sparks and hissed as if someone were whispering to him. And if you can believe it, a tree grew amid those flames. An apple tree grew from the engulfed ruins. It grew ten feet tall, and it produced fruit. The fire eventually went out and from that day forward, the story served as a warning. It reminded the children to never take their parents for granted because Johnny would come back with his apple seeds."

Madison glanced over at Mary Beth's strange apple tree by her fence. The limbs moved on their own as if the wind was causing them to dance. There was no wind blowing. Madison turned his gaze back to Mary Beth. She had vacated her rocking chair and was crouched liked a gargoyle next to him. Mary Beth's eyes blazed crimson as she snatched Maddison's arm and growled. "You're next!"

Madison jumped as he peered down at his arm. Quarter sized holes were forming. Jerking his arm away, Madison jumped from the porch, leaving behind his ball.

Mary Beth cackled as she watched Madison shrieking as he ran. Maybe that is why the children thought she was a witch.

Nocturnal Awakening

In the end, everyone must sleep, right? I mean, I lay there tossing and turning in my bed night after night. I hoped the medicine my physician prescribed would have some effect. I have taken them for a while now and nothing has changed. A doctor once advised me to place a Tick-Tock clock near my bed. He suggested the ticking noise would help to soothe me to sleep. It ended up driving me insane. Its ticking pierced the darkness like tiny little knives stabbing my brain one tick at a time.

I can't help but feel like the dark is a vast tomb with no air and no noise. I placed a rotating fan at the end of my bed. The air it circulated cut through the claustrophobia. Without it, my mind thinks I am buried alive.

I tried Light Therapy. I must admit; it was weird. I stared at an intense white light for thirty minutes before bedtime. Health nuts online said it would help develop natural melatonin in my brain. Maybe I'm just hard-headed because it didn't work. It did nothing but make me see tiny white squares in the dark until they vanished.

I thought my problem was all in my head. I called a psychologist. At first, my shrink and I spoke about the past. I couldn't find anything that would make me afraid of the dark or not want to sleep. He tried to hypnotize me, but it didn't work. I am no longer a patient of his.

My mother used to suggest I was a tormented soul, and that is why I couldn't sleep. There may be some truth to that but just like insomnia; there is no magic pill to cure that either. As a child, my mother brought me warm milk and read a book to me until I fell asleep. I smiled to myself as I rolled back my blankets and sat up in the dark. I decided to try my mother's old tried-and-true method, warm milk. It couldn't hurt anything; I have tried everything else.

As I swiveled my legs out of bed, I realized how awful I felt. I was sticky and hot from the tossing I had done under my blankets. I reached out into the dark, found the lamp, and twisted on the switch. I found a hair tie on my side table. Pulling my hair up with both hands, I arranged my knotted mess into a bun on top of my head. I stood up and headed to the kitchen. I bumped my way through the darkened living room, and I somehow found the kitchen. I turned on the light.

Pulling open the refrigerator door, I welcomed the refreshing air that floated over my flushed skin. I glanced through the refrigerator's contents. I quickly realized that I was out of milk. I racked my brain to remember the stores that remained open late at night. I hate convenient store shopping. The previous two attempts were a disappointment. The first time I tried it, the milk had gone sour. I found out the hard way after I poured myself a cup of milk. Chunks of white milk flopped out of the carton instead of creamy milk. The second time I tried a convenience store, the milk tasted like plastic. I swore off convenient stores for good. I suddenly thought of Sunny Mart. Last year, they revealed their plans to stay open twenty-four hours a day, seven days a week.

After heading upstairs to my bedroom and changing my clothes, I headed out the door. I felt odd walking outside at three in the morning. "Maybe this is how people come up with those vampire stories," I thought to myself. As quickly as the notion crossed my mind, I wished I hadn't considered something so ghoulish. Quickening my steps to my car, I jumped in. I locked my car doors as fast as I could. I searched around me, and nobody was afoot. Laughing at myself, I started the ignition. I backed out of my driveway and headed for Sunny Mart.

The highway was empty. I didn't pass a single car on the way there, not even a police car. The isolation made me feel uneasy. Continuing out of desperation for warm milk and sleep, I turned into Sunny Mart. It surprised me to see a few cars parked there. I slipped into a vacant spot near the door and climbed out of my car. I headed inside.

The store was bright and active. A smiling elderly woman cheerfully greeted me and gave me a flyer about current sales. I accepted one and moved further into the store. If I had not just checked my watch, I would have believed it was the middle of the day instead of three-thirty in the morning. I strolled around and saw a woman shopping for clothes. Someone was weighing produce, and a man was shopping for a fishing rod. There were a few individuals standing in line, waiting to have their goods rung up at the register. I felt like I was in a strange realm where time stood still, and it was always daytime.

Shaking off the ominous feeling, I wandered to the dairy aisle where they stored the milk. I found my favorite brand and headed to the cash register. As I walked, I noticed the store had an extensive book aisle. I decided to grab something to read. I needed all the help I could get.

Something in my gut told me not to stick around, but I had nothing to read at home. I was desperate for something to make me sleepy. I glanced at the selection of novels. I found one about vampires and I thought about the car ordeal. I passed. I spotted a nice romance story. Now that was my area. As I read the synopsis of the book, I noticed a youthful woman looking at me with a smirk.

"I've read that one and trust me, it's not that great." She said with a grin.

"Thanks, I'll take that into consideration." I responded. I secretly hoped she would go away.

"I have read just about everything here. I can't sleep. This is the only store that is open all the time." She replied as she adjusted her shopping basket on her arm. She pushed back her flaming red hair from her shoulders before picking up a paperback. "Now this one... is a page turner. It's about a mountain man who discovers gold and the love of his life. The way the writer described the mountains was incredible. It helped me to unwind." She added with a sigh. She handed me the book.

I looked it over and put it back. "No thanks, I think I will stick with this one." I tried to give her a hint. I turned my back to the peculiar girl.

"You must be new to the late-night shopping experience. This store is outstanding. They love us insomniacs." She said with a giggle.

The girls' eyes grew large with excitement as she went on. "One night, I wandered around and sampled the pastries without paying for them. I played on their game systems in the toy aisle all night long and they never kicked me out."

I twisted back to face the chatty girl. "Why would they do that?" I replied, feeling a little confused.

"If they booted out individuals like me, the people who can't sleep, how would their store stay alive? Try it! You would have so much fun!"

"No thanks. You have insomnia?"

"Oh yeah, I haven't slept all night since I was a kid. I have tried everything, and nothing works. I came here one night when I couldn't sleep. I discovered I felt better just being here. You know what I mean?"

"I guess... I don't know." I answered, feeling strange by the young woman's behavior again.

I drifted away from the odd girl and roamed around the store. It couldn't hurt. After all, I didn't feel sleepy. I felt more awake than I did before I left the house. As I headed to the clothing aisle, I sensed the strange girl behind me. I spun around, and she was so close we could have kissed. I backed up a step.

"Oops, I'm sorry; I just realized something. I didn't catch your name. I'm Angel." She stated as she reached out her hand. I accepted it reluctantly.

"I'm Juliette."

"Ooh, like Romeo and Juliette? How romantic. No wonder you read those novels."

"Um, look, I don't want to be impolite, but I prefer to shop alone. You understand, right?"

"Oh, I get it, you're like most of us on our first night here... antisocial." She responded with a sympathetic smile.

"Yeah, I guess. I just like to shop by myself, so if you don't mind." I repeated, as I struggled to walk away again.

Angel laughed as she followed close behind. "You're just like Tommy over there." She stated as she pointed to a man I had observed earlier shopping for fishing poles. "At first, he was antisocial too, but he came around. He sure is a fighter." She added as she studied Tommy from a distance. "And look at Mrs. Andrews, she cussed and hollered until she admitted her destiny. Oh, gosh... and over there by the bikinis, that's Dee Dee; she is still ignoring us." Dee Dee looked up at us and crisscrossed her arms with a scowl. I had a sagging feeling in my gut.

"What are you trying to say, Angel? You talk as if we are stuck here." I replied, a little nervous.

"Well, you are." She answered matter of fact.

"Look, I have had just about enough of you. If you don't leave me alone, I will get a manager, or I'll call the cops."

"Cellphones don't work in here and if you hadn't noticed, there are no managers on the floor." She grinned, but this time with a hint of fear. "Look, the sooner you accept it, the better it will be on you."

"You're full of crap." I replied as I reached into my handbag and fished out my cellphone. Just as she said, there was no signal. I wandered around the store to look for a manager. Angel skipped merrily behind me like a child. I turned to look at her. "Leave me alone!" I walked faster with the purpose to locate someone. Just as Angel had reported, there was no manager on the floor. I spun around to confront her again, but she had vanished.

I headed to the register with my book and my milk. I stood in line behind an aged man. As I waited, I repeatedly looked over my shoulder, hoping Angel wasn't there waiting to ambush me. The elderly man gathered up his items. He shuffled away, but he didn't walk out of the store. Instead, he strolled over to a bench and sat down. I concluded he must be waiting for someone.

The checkout lady was smiling at me. She thanked me for shopping at Sunny Mart as she scanned my items. She loaded my book and milk into a plastic bag and handed them to me. I looked at the total. It read, amount owed, zero. I stared at her in bewilderment. "How much, miss?"

"Your money is no good here, Juliette." She answered with a smile as she pushed the bag into my hand.

"What are you talking about? Am I on a hidden comedy show?" I replied as I searched around for people with cameras just waiting to jump out at me.

"I don't understand." The checkout lady responded with a stiff smile.

"I can't just accept this without paying."

"You belong here, Juliette. Please take it." She answered in a panicked voice.

At that moment, the intercom boomed with strange elevator music playing gently in the background. "Welcome, Juliette, to Sunny Mart, where it's always a sunny shopping experience. Take in the sights of the store. From our exciting toy department to our fabulous women's wear! Relax in our camping section, where you can take a nap on our hammocks or in one of our roll-up sleeping bags!" The male voice said in his best game show accent.

"Who are you?" I answered as I searched around, seeking to discover the origin of the voice.

"I am the answer to your insomnia!"

"Oh yeah, and what answer do you have?" I yelled up at the ceiling.

"A never-ending night! Here, you will never fret about going to sleep because, well… here, you will never sleep!" The game show voice resounded through the store. The voice ended his speech with a sickening laugh. I glanced around and noticed the patrons were staring at me. For the first time, I could see the shadowy circles under their eyes. Their clothes dangled from their emaciated frames. They looked pale. It was as if their skin had never tasted the sunlight. They looked desperate for me to rescue them. My bag slipped from my hands. When the milk struck the floor, the plastic broke open. Milk splashed over my legs and feet. The icy liquid woke me from my terror.

"Oops, clean up in the checkout line!" The creepy game show host's voice announced over the microphone. His giggle was fortified with madness.

I slid in the spilled milk and fell, but somehow, I scrambled up onto my feet. I dashed towards the front door. The once smiling elderly woman who greeted me settled in front of the door as if to intercept me. I figured it was do or die. I rushed at her like a linebacker. Slamming into her slender frame as rough as I could, the bones in her ribs made a loud crunching noise as we went down to the floor. I jumped to my feet as she clutched her sides and recoiled in agony. The electronic doors didn't open when I stepped in front of the sensor.

"Come on, Juliette. You know you can't leave. What is out there waiting for you, an empty house with an empty bed? You're with people who understand you. Come, Juliette; come be a part of my wonderland." His tone became deeper with each word he spoke, giving up the game show facade. "Come to me, Juliette. You will never worry about sleeping again. Take command of your weakness. Let go of the uncertainty. The headaches you have from not getting your eight hours... gone." His voice became tender as he pressed on. "Juliette, let go. Come to me and let go." I reached down and pinched my arm to snap myself away from his hypnotic tone.

"No!" I shifted to the door and kicked the glass. Every time it broke, it would mend itself. I searched for a release latch. Of course, this hellhole didn't have one. I found the crease where the doors opened. I wedged my fingers into the crack and pulled. It gave, so I tugged harder. It opened just wide enough to slide my body through. I glanced over my shoulder and the skeletal people gradually made their way toward me. They looked like zombies walking toward their prey. I slipped my body between the doors. The doors pushed against my abdomen. I could barely breathe. I was trapped.

"If you give in... I'll open the doors, Juliette. Do you concede?" The mysterious voice asked over the intercom as the doors pushed in. I could hear rushing in my ears as I started to pass out. I nodded my head yes with what strength I had left. The doors flung open. I crumpled to the floor. As I attempted to catch my breath, I worked to drag myself to my feet. Instead, I felt myself being hauled back into the store. The doors slammed shut behind me.

The little elderly lady was back on her feet, smiling as if nothing had taken place. She helped me to my feet, and she handed me a flyer. "Welcome to Sunny Mart." She said with a pleasant smile shining through her gaunt face.

I peered around and everybody had returned to their shopping. Tommy was at the fishing and camping section, hoping he would go camping someday. Dee Dee was eyeing bathing suits. She acted as if she were searching for a bikini for the vacation of a lifetime. Angel was skipping like a little schoolgirl around the store with a basket full of free things.

The old woman gave me a shopping cart, and I accepted it miserably. I don't know what kind of hell I have stepped into. I only know that my insomnia, that once made me a prisoner in my home, now made me a hostage of the Sunny Mart. Maybe this was a purgatory for the tormented souls my mother used to talk about.

What will happen to us?

Will we ever sleep again?

I mean, in the end everyone must sleep... right?

Tales from the edge of death

"Why do I do this to myself? I hate funerals. The sun is beating down on my head. I don't even know half the people here. Hell, I don't even know my deceased aunt well. I'm going to remind myself later to yell at my sister. She always does this to me. She made me feel guilty for not showing up to all the burials in the family. I have a life, an actual life as a journalist. I worked hard to be where I am today. I work for a prominent newspaper, The Looking Glass Gazette. I have been writing for the paper for five years now. I moved up to the special feature reporter. I'm proud of my achievements. Who was she to make me feel bad? I have to get out of here," I thought to myself as I glanced around the cemetery.

The July heat had made the grass brown, and it crunched under my feet. It was an old graveyard. It's been in the family for centuries. They buried everyone in the Johnson family there. My parents are buried there. There are a few names I don't recognize on the stones. Some headstones are so old you can't read the names. I used to frequent the family graveyard when I was a teenager to sneak a cigarette. After mom and dad passed, I just couldn't deal with this place anymore. I wandered away from the service over to my parent's graves. It's been ten years since they died in that terrible car accident.

I passed my fingertips over their names, Edna and Bill Johnson. I felt a knot swell in my throat as I reached into my handbag to retrieve my cigarettes. I shifted my focus so I wouldn't break down. The funeral looked like it was wrapping up. "Maybe I can get to my car with no one noticing me," I thought with optimism.

I strode with my head down at a vigorous trot. It was too late. Aunt Martha had spotted me. "Susan! Oh, Susan, how surprising to see you! Oh, and at such a dreadful time. I can't believe my sister is gone." Aunt Martha said as she swabbed at her eye with a wrinkled tissue.

"Aunt Martha, it's nice to see you, too. I hated to hear about Aunt Kate. Are you ok?"

"Oh yes, her passing was peaceful. The cancer took her quick, but she had made peace with the good lord years ago. Kate told me she was ready. You know, the peculiar part about her death was when it was just she and I at the hospice. I knew she only had a few hours left. I stayed with her so she wouldn't pass alone." Aunt Martha sniffed and mopped her nose again. This time, she blew it so hard that it made a trumpet sound.

Aunt Martha gave me a watery smile as she shoved her napkin in her dress pocket. I didn't want to hear anymore, but she pushed on, anyway. "It was three o'clock in the morning. She was sleeping peacefully. Then abruptly she woke up with this beautiful smile. She turned her sweet face to me, then to the corner of the room. She held out her arms and opened her palms wide as if she were about to hug someone. Then she spoke out to the corner of the room and said, yes take me home. After the words left her mouth, her arms dropped, and she was gone." Aunt Martha burst into renewed sobs and a family member that I did not remember came over to soothe her.

I hotfooted it into my car. This time I made it. I guess I'm not the only one trying to get out quick. The cars were backed up from the cemetery all the way to the main highway. Realizing it would take forever to get out of the graveyard, I elected to call the office. I dreaded it.

These days my boss, Mr. Shultz, has been thinking up my features for me. It was his way of asserting my articles have been crap. I need to have a story in mind before I called. Let's face it; I have been out of ideas for a while. I glanced around the cemetery, and it struck me. I picked up my cellphone and dialed the numbers. "Hello, Looking Glass Gazette. How may I direct your call?"

"Hey, Amy, its Susan. Can you put me through to Mr. Shultz?"

"Sure, hold please."

"Hello?" Mr. Shultz said in his rugged tone.

"Mr. Shultz, it's Susan."

"Susan! Just the gal I needed to talk to. I got an excellent idea for your column this week. It's about the school field trip..."

"Mr. Shultz, I have a story idea this week." I answered as I quickly butted in.

"Oh? Well, let's hear it." He replied with curiosity in his voice.

"Ok, as you know, I just left my aunt's funeral. It made me think about the afterlife. Some people show signs that the afterlife exists. I wanted to get stories from people who witnessed their loved one's drawing their last breath. I want to ask them if their relative saw or said anything before they passed. There are many reports of people seeing death or angels coming for them. I think it would be a fascinating article." I became silent as I listened to Mr. Shultz breathing over the phone.

"Well, I'll tell you what, you write me up something and I'll have a peek at it. If it's not what I'm searching for, you will have to write about the field trip."

"Yes, sir!" I hung up the phone with excitement. I finally had something he might appreciate. As traffic moved, I plotted my story.

The next day, I headed to my office. I searched for Pam; she's the busybody of the Gazette. She knows everybody in town. I knew she could hook me up with people who could share their experiences with me. I looked in the only place a food addict would be. The snack machines. "Hey, Pam." I said to Pam's plump rear end in the air in front of the snack machine.

Pam fished out her honey bun and swung around. A slight smirk appeared on her dimpled cheeks. Her double chin grew fuller. "What is it, Susan? You realize I don't owe you anymore favors. As I recall, you owe me." She announced as she opened her sweet treat. Taking a giant bite as she enjoyed my misery, she rolled her eyes at me and sighed. "Alright, maybe one more; what is it?" She added as she chewed like a cow.

"Thanks, Pam, you're the greatest! Ok, so I have this story about the afterlife. I need people to talk to that have attended their loved one's death. Maybe the deceased said something as they were passing. Know anyone like that?"

"Let me think." Pam said as she finished her honey bun.

Pam finished her last bite slowly for dramatic effect. "Yeah, I guess I know a few, in my family. Let me write down their numbers and addresses so you can go out there.

I'll set them up, ok? And this time, Susan, give me credit in the article for the help. You know I love to see my name in the paper."

"Sounds good to me."

"Permit me today to call everybody and set it up. You can head out tomorrow, ok? I'll e-mail you who and where to go."

I got up the next morning and I reviewed my e-mail. Bless her heart, Pam came through. There were only three people listed. I had to make it work. I studied the names. The first name on the list was Janelle. She lived on Burbank Street. She lost her husband to colon cancer. I printed out the e-mail and got dressed. After I dressed, I grabbed my tape recorder and headed out the door. I don't know if anyone used recorders anymore. I discovered I could be more accurate in my quotes if I played the tape later.

As I pulled into Janelle's driveway, I took in the sights of her home. She lived in a charming white cottage with blue shutters on the windows. Flowers were planted as far as the eye could see. She had a white picket fence to complete the picturesque scenery. The white curtain in the window moved to the side as I strolled up the tiny stone walkway to Janelle's door. Before I could knock, she opened the door. "I hope I didn't startle you. My little girl is asleep." Janelle said with a gentle smile. "You must be Susan, please come in."

I stepped into her home. I mentally compared her home to my apartment. My place looked like a pigsty compared to her fairytale dream home. Her house was immaculate, with its polished wood floors and white sofa. I couldn't believe a little girl lived there, too. There were too many breakable crystal vases around for a child to live there. I sat down on the edge of the sofa and drew out my tape record-er. I pressed the record button. "Thank you for allowing me to come into your home and for sharing with me such a personal story."

"Well, when Pam called, it was a surprise. She didn't believe me when I told her the story of Tom's death. Do you believe in life after death, Susan?" she asked with hope etched on her face as she sat down next to me.

"Well, that's what I am trying to find out. I'm doing research for an article I am writing for The Looking Glass Gazette. After my aunt's funeral, I wanted to dig a little deeper."

"I'm sorry to hear of your loss." Janelle looked over at a silver-framed picture. "Tom was a remarkable man. He was a firefighter for seven years before they diagnosed him with colon cancer. He fought so hard, but the cancer was just too strong. The morning he passed; I was hold-ing his hand. We spoke about the day we got married and the day Destiny was born. We prayed together for the last time…"

Janelle's eyes filled with tears. "Then suddenly he looked up to the ceiling, and he asked me if I could hear that. I asked him what he heard. He said, the wings flut-tering. I studied him and he had such a beautiful grin on his face. He asked me if I could hear the music. It was at that moment that I realized he was hearing heaven. Before I could react, he slipped into a coma. Within the hour, he died. I was heartbroken, but I felt peace." Janelle grabbed a tissue from a box on the coffee table as she went on.

"I thought, maybe, just maybe, that was angel's wings. I think he heard the music of heaven calling him home." Janelle smiled to herself at the thought. After the conversation was over, Janelle invited me to her church and asked me to keep in touch. I couldn't help but note how graceful Janelle was as she summoned her painful moment. I didn't think I could be as calm as Janelle under that kind of grief.

The next stop was a nursing home on Veterans Boulevard. This time, it was a nurse. She was Pam's cousin. I wandered into the cold nursing home, wishing I had brought a coat. It was the middle of July; who remembers a coat? The nursing home smelled like bleach and arthritis cream. The nurses dressed in their scrubs with various designs on the shirts. Some had pleasant smiles, while others had the expression of stressed concentration. I stepped over to the nurses' station and asked for Nurse Angela. An elderly lady with a volunteer tag pinned to her sweater stood up and led me to an office. It was scarcely big enough for a desk, much less a chair for me to sit on. Angela looked up from her laptop monitor and held out her hand. "Susan, nice to meet you. Pam has told me all about you. Please have a seat."

Angela glanced around me and called out. "Donna, could you shut the door, please?" After the door shut, Donna was gone, and it was just me and Nurse Angela. She was an older lady. Time had been rough on her, but she had a pleasant smile. "So, you wish to listen to my tales? I seldom reveal what I see here, but I'm growing old. I'm leaving their names out if you don't mind."

"Of course not, thank you for taking the time to talk with me." I replied, as I drew out my tape recorder and pressed the record button. "Please go ahead."

"Well, as a nurse, you encounter many things. I am here at all hours. The first death I witnessed was a woman about the age of forty. I'll call her Carrie. She was a hefty girl. She suffered from uterine cancer. Well, one night I could hear her yelling down the hall. I went running to her room, and she was screaming, help me, help me, my feet are on fire. I tried to soothe her, but she just kept wailing. I thought I could fan her feet to cool her down. Well, I pulled back the blankets from her feet and blood was all over the bed. She was bleeding out. I looked up, and she passed right in front of my eyes. When I spoke of it to my mother, she claimed the woman was entering hell. I don't know about that."

Angela shook her head as she worked to shake off the memory. "Then there was a man. I'll call him Walter. Walter was a tough country boy until he became sick. He had been exposed to some chemicals in the Vietnam War. For weeks he would go in and out of comas. When he would wake up, he would talk to someone in the armchair next to his bed. One night, I asked him who he was speaking to. He told me he was talking to his mother. His mother had been deceased for twenty years. His wife claimed Walter said, I'm coming, momma, just before he died. The list goes on and on."

"So, you believe there is life after death?"

"Yes, I do, sweetheart." She replied with a soft smile.

After a brief round of questions, I left her office feeling frustrated. It made me question everything I thought I knew about death. I trudged down the corridor from Nurse Angela's office. I noticed a door open to a patient's room. I peeked in and discovered a slight elderly lady lying on a hospital bed. She was attached to tubes and wires fastened to instruments that beeped to a steady rhythm. I don't know why, but I went in and sat next to her bed. I stared at her frail little face, and I thought of my mother. She had died before I could say goodbye.

There were no machines, no last-minute decisions to be made to save her life. She was gone in an instant and my father followed behind her into the great unknown. It surprised me to see the little elderly lady opening her eyes. She stared at the wall before turning to look at me. "He's here." She announced as she shifted back to look at the wall.

Fear rushed through my body. I knew something was there waiting for me to look. I gathered my courage and turned my head. My sweaty hands clutched the arms of the chair. I felt as if I would throw up. A towering, hooded figure stood by the wall. Its body was translucent. It was almost as if it were a part of the wall.

It stood with its hooded face pointed in my direction. Then it spoke. "It is not your time. Fear not." It spoke in a stern male tone.

I swallowed hard and found my voice. "Who are you?"

"You know who I am, Susan."

"Why are you haunting me?"

"I am not here to torment you. I am here to collect this soul and take her home."

"But… why are you showing yourself to me?"

"I overheard your discussion with the soul called, Angela. I became curious why you were asking questions about me."

"About you? I don't understand?" Susan shook her head in bewilderment.

"You know who I am, Susan, and you know what I do. You ask questions of the souls I gathered. Why?"

Tears ran down my face. The truth poured forth. "My parents; why did you take them? I needed them, and you took them. Why?" I sobbed.

"I do not collect souls because I desire it to be so. It is their time. I owe you no other answer."

"You owe me. You took away my joy when you took them from me. At least tell me what their last words were."

"Their last words were of you. They said they loved you."

I sniffed and dried my tears. I had to ask one more time, even though I knew who he was. "Who are you?"

He stretched out his arm, and a pale white hand appeared from under the robe. "You know who I am." He replied as he pointed at me. Before I realized what was going on, he gripped his robe and flung it open. A light brighter than the sunlight gleamed through the room. Beside me, I could hear the little elderly ladies' machine beeping fast, and then a long beep followed. I covered my eyes and head, but the light wouldn't go out. I dared to peek at the lighted figure illuminating the room. As I narrowed my eyes, I could make out the figure of a magnificent man. His skin was so transparent that I could practically see his skeleton. His arms were reaching out to the elderly lady. He glanced over at me, and the light became brighter.

Hiding my eyes once more until the light had diminished, I heard feet running into the room. I opened my eyes. I let them readjust to the room's natural lighting. Looking up, I saw Nurse Angela staring at me with wide eyes. "Susan? Is that you?" She said cautiously.

"What do you mean, is it me? We were just talking like five minutes ago." I answered as I blinked her face into focus.

"But… but… your hair; it's snow white." She declared with amazement. She fished a compact mirror out of her pocket and held it up to my face. I couldn't believe it was me looking back through the glass. The hair style was right, but the color was as white as paper. The face wore a shocked expression. It turned and blinked as I did. But this face was the hue of wood ash, like a gaunt zombie. I did not know what happened to me.

There was something out there other than the death of the human body. The soul went somewhere after it died. I knew that now. I reached a shaking hand to my cellphone and dialed the phone number to my bosses' office. "Amy… get me Mr. Shultz." I suppose she heard the stress in my tone because she transferred me over to his office immediately.

"Susan! What you got for me?"

"Sir, I can't do the article. I'm sorry."

"What happened? I thought it was a good one." He replied, full of fake concern.

"I can't explain. I just can't do it." I answered in a shaking voice.

"Well… I guess it's the field trip story for you!"

The Elevator

You make a million decisions every day. What time to wake up or how long to shower. Which direction will you to take on the way to work? Should I force down breakfast or have an early lunch? I could go on and on with the millions of possibilities. I never thought about the different directions my life could have gone or where it was headed. Since I was a child, money was the boss in the house. My father, God rest his soul, was a baker. He owned his own bakery. Our family lived above the shop in a tight quartered apartment.

Dad declared, "You mark my words Princess, nothing and I mean nothing can work out your troubles like money can. Never depend on family or friends. And remember, there is no such thing as the kindness of strangers. People will let you down." He would smile his sweetest smile and pet me on the head. I used to think that was his way of being playful. Maybe he just wanted me to feel inspired to go to college. I didn't figure out his intention until I became independent.

The intelligence of his remarks came to light after I moved out on my own at eighteen. My first electric bill came in the mail at the same time as my water bill. My refrigerator was practically empty. I was working at a pizza restaurant. I suppose they assumed I could survive off the crap they paid me. I had to determine what was essential, food, water or lights? Lights and water won the toss up. I ate the pizza some customers did not pick up or slices they left on the tables. I broke down and went home crying to my father. It astonished me how tender and understanding he was. He looked at me with a caring smile and hugged me. Next, he carried my bags to my old room. My father recited his famous line about money solving all your problems before leaving me in my silent room to think. As my pride throbbed with misery, I understood I had to hit the books and make a ton of money.

Four years and a state certification test later, I was a certified accountant. How could I know that one day I would climb into an elevator and encounter death? My life and four other lives flashed before my eyes. I'll start from the beginning.

I was lucky to land an internship at West & Johnson, Inc. At first, I delivered mail. I worked my way up. I applied for every job posting for an accountant. A year later, I was doing business with my own clients. With my first paycheck, I opened a savings account. Eight years later, I had a glorious life. My favorite routine was to walk up the 12 flights of stairs to get to my office. It was a habit I picked up when I realized sitting down all day working without a break was making my clothes tighter. I enjoyed taking the stairs. It gave me the extra thirty minutes of exercise I needed. Of course, I had to leave the house thirty minutes early, but it was worth it.

One morning, I woke up with a start. My cellphone was ringing off the hook. I glanced over at my clock, and it was blinking 12:00 AM over and over. A storm had affected the power.

I normally set my alarm on my cellphone when storms came. Engrossed in a steamy romance novel I had picked up at the grocery store, I neglected to set the alarm. I snatched the phone with sleepy fingers and fumbled for the answer key. "Hello?"

"Sara? Oh, thank God! I thought you had been murdered!"

"Don't be so dramatic, Tara. The storm knocked out my power. No big deal." I answered as I rubbed my eyes.

Tara was my assistant. The best girl for the job, but she could be a drama queen in the worst times possible. "Well, the big boss is asking for you. He keeps coming into your office every thirty minutes and checking his wristwatch. What Should I tell him, Sara?" She replied in a breathy tone.

"Tell him the truth and that I am leaving now." I said in my most soothing voice, hoping it would appease her.

"Ok. Hurry, Sara. You realize we will be fired if you tick off the boss." She declared before she hung up the phone. Pulling the phone away from my ear, I glared at it for a minute. I suppose I thought my expression of revulsion would burn through the phone lines and slap Tara around. I did not know what Tara was talking about. Her job was secure. Tara didn't like the spotlight on her when the "Big" boss was watching for me. I rolled my eyes at the thought.

As I sat up, I let my eyes adjust to the morning light. I peeked at my watch; ten-thirty. Jumping up, I flung open my closest door. I seized the closest suit jacket and trousers to match. I thumbed through my blouses and snatched my blue silk shirt. In record time, I was dressed. I dashed to the bathroom and managed a rush job on my makeup. I brushed my teeth and hair before cramming my feet into my heels. In a clumsy manor, I snagged my briefcase and keys. I was out the door and on my way to work.

As I pulled into my private parking spot, I realized I would have to take the elevator; it was something I despised. I must admit it, I'm claustrophobic. My claustrophobia became worse when someone with strong cologne got onto the elevator with me. It clogged the air and made it difficult to breathe. I shook off the dread and clambered out of my car. I headed into the building that I considered my second home. My heart raced as I trudged to the elevator. Four individuals were standing in front of the first elevator in the lobby. There were three elevators. This one opened first. I resisted the impulse to wait for the next one. I was late and this could save a few precious seconds.

An elderly woman shuffled towards the elevator. She would have heavy perfume on. In a panic, I reached out and hit the "close door" switch. I watched as her determined expression on her face slid off and was replaced with a look of surprise.

In the metal reflection of the closing doors, I could see the glances of disapproval. "So what. They don't pay my bills," I thought to myself. "I'm twenty-nine years old now. I have earned my right to keep undesirable people away," I thought once more with a sneer. I looked each person in the eyes in the reflection. I gave them an expression that implied, "You have something to say?" Everyone, one by one, dropped their gaze. They went back to pretending they were the only person in the elevator. I almost let out a snicker when my ear detected a slight ticking noise. I glanced around to see if anybody was wearing a disturbingly loud watch. It spooked me to discover everyone else was searching for the same commotion. My heart dropped as I realized it was happening above us.

I could feel the elevator slowing down. It moaned and shuttered as it struggled to complete its function to get us to the last floor. I glanced up at the numbers that show what floor we reached. Just before the light went out, it flashed 12. Our building did not have a thirteenth floor, for obvious reasons. With a last heave, the elevator came to a standstill. I sat frozen, staring at a woman in the reflection. She had an expression of terror on her face. My face emptied of all color when I realized it was my face I was looking at. My worst nightmare was coming true.

I jumped when I saw a long arm reach past me and moved me aside. I glanced over to discover a youthful man. He could not have been over twenty-five. He looked as if he was dressed to go to church. His necktie was a little too tight. "Excuse me, there should be a box to call for help." He stated with confidence. I watched him fumble around the glowing keypad and pull open a door. It had an old-fashioned phone in it. The young man brought the phone to his ear and waited until he heard someone answer. "Yes, sir; I'm stuck in elevator number one." He listened again. "Yes, sir; I believe it broke down between floors eleven and..."

Before he could complete his sentence, we felt the elevator drop with a rush. A blood-curdling scream erupted from my mouth. I felt the air rushing out of my lungs as a force flung me to the floor. The elevator had stopped. I gripped the side of the elevator wall with trembling hands and dragged myself to a sitting position. I glanced around at the others, who were doing the same thing. A young girl was holding her head as a red egg-shaped knot formed under her fingers.

The young man, clinging to the phone, pulled the receiver back to his ear. "Are you still there? We just fell..." He closed his eyes, seeking to concentrate. "I don't know how many floors. The emergency breaks must have caught." He listened to the voice on the line as he worked to steady his breathing. "Ok. Please hurry." As he hung up the phone, he looked around. "The guy on the phone said he called 911 and maintenance. He said try to remain calm and don't bounce the elevator."

"What? Like we are going to jump up and down and party until they get here?" I responded with sarcasm before I could stop myself.

"Look, I'm just repeating what he said, ok?"

"Sorry." I grumbled.

We waited for what felt like an eternity. I glanced at my wristwatch; two o'clock. I brushed a jittery hand across my moist brow. I guessed my boss was ready to terminate me at that point. "My cellphone," I thought to myself. I moved to search in my briefcase when I recalled my rush journey out of the front door. My cellphone at that very minute was resting on its charger on the nightstand. I set my head back on the elevator wall with a painful thump. "Perfect." I said with misery.

"What?" the young man spoke with concern.

I looked up with surprise. "My cellphone is at home. I can't call my boss."

"Are you afraid you'll get fired?"

"I was running late this morning because of the storm last night. Now, I'm going to die before I can explain what happened to me." I replied with a bitter snort.

"That's just terrific. Did you think maybe we could live through this?" I glanced over to see a teenage girl at least sixteen years old with her arms crisscrossed over her chest. She was throwing me a glare that she set aside for her parents when she thought she was being treated unfairly.

"What's your name?" I answered with caution. I didn't want a teenage drama on my hands.

"Autumn." she replied with her brow furrowed.

"Well, Autumn, I was being sarcastic. That is how most adults deal with a troublesome situation." I said in a smooth schoolteacher tone. Autumn rolled her eyes.

"Well, what if we die? What if...?" said the young man as his eyes brimmed with tears.

"What's your name?" I whispered.

"Maxwell. Well, Max to my friends." He responded with a sniff. He reached up and loosened his tie. "I can't believe I'm in this position. I didn't even want to be here in the first place. If my old man wasn't such a dictator, I'd be traveling around the world right now. Instead, I'm trapped in a metal coffin."

"Look, Max, we will not die." I suggested that for his benefit, not mine. Truth be told, I was as scared as a small child. But somehow, I felt strong.

I have overheard people say that when you face a life-or-death situation, your inner strength comes out to guide you. "They will fix this old heap and we will be back to our worker bee lives." Max almost smiled and shrugged.

"This is a sign." A dreamy voice in the corner spoke up. It was the young girl with the knot on her head. "Hi, I'm Izzy. Well, it's Elizabeth, friends call me Izzy."

Izzy was a modern day hippy. She had a long skirt that had a rainbow of colors on it. Her hair hung down to her waistline. She wore little to no makeup. She smelled like lavender and spices.

"What sign are you talking about?" I asked with curiosity.

"Well, all my life, I have believed in living life to the fullest. Some days are full of questions about whom, what, and when. Then you're stuck wondering how you are going to achieve the answers. Sometimes it takes a crisis to show you the way. Most of the time, the answer is so simple you can't see it until confronted with unwanted circumstances. For example, when I was in college, I was miserable. My parents wanted me to be a doctor. I didn't want to be in the medical world. I worked in a deli to pay for my schoolbooks, and I loved it. One day I went to a party with a friend, we were in a head on collision. I almost died. It put everything into perspective. I realized the only time I was happy was when I was at the deli. After my painful recovery, I opened my sandwich shop. That's why I'm here. I was delivering sandwiches. I never would have thought this would happen. When I get out of here, I will make peace with my parents. It hasn't been the same between us since I left school." Izzy sighed and looked down for a moment before smiling to herself.

"Well, I, for one, will never get on an elevator again. I mean, what century is this? Elevators have been around for like… well, forever! Don't you think they would have mastered it by now?" Autumn said with a huff.

"If I live through this, I am going to give up trying to please my father." Max added, deep in thought. "I just needed to see the look of you did it, son on my father's face. Why couldn't he say, I'm proud of you? He's this hot shot attorney. He told me I was going to follow in his footsteps. I devoted four years to Harvard. Four long years. Was that enough? Of course not. If I live through this, I'm going to leave this corporate world. I'm going to become a photographer and travel around the world. No more people pleasing B.S. I'm going to live the way I want to." He stated as he looked at me with a satisfied grin.

I glanced over in the other corner and observed a woman quietly gripping her handbag tight to her chest. She didn't look like she worked in my building. She dressed like a soccer mom. There was a storm brewing in her eyes. Tornadoes swirled with tormenting thoughts in her mind. I became curious enough to talk to her. "What about you?"

"Huh?" the shy woman answered with a start. "Me?"

"Yeah, what's your name?"

"Joan." she responded with strained anxiety. "I suppose if I live through this, I'll continue to do what I set out to do today." It was a safe answer. She peered around and realized everybody was expecting her to continue. "Well, it's not a big story. I just came here hoping to save my farm. My husband doesn't know I'm here." Her eyes watered. "Our dairy farm took a financial blow when the economy was having trouble. We recovered, but it was taking a while to get caught up on the mortgage payments. We are five thousand dollars behind and the bank said they were going to foreclose. I didn't understand. We have been behind before and the bank worked with us. I did a little digging. I found out a major retailer wants our land to build a new supercenter and outlet mall. They offered the bank at least half a million dollars over market value. My husband wants to sell, but I hired a lawyer. Watching my husband's anguish over giving up his dream of being a farmer… it's just too much to carry. Now, if I die, he'll never know how much that farm meant to me. I complained so much about the hours and how the cows were just pets to him. I was such an idiot." Joan placed her face in her hands and covered the tears she shed.

Everything grew quiet after that. We sat in silence with our thoughts. I almost opened my mouth to share my story when the elevator came to life like a vibrating animal. We stood up and cheered. We embraced as if we had known each other our entire lives. The doors flew open and refreshing air engulfed the elevator. I closed my eyes and let reality set in. I opened my eyes and watched everyone reunite with family and friends. Autumn ran to her mom and embraced her with a whispered, I love you. Max walked quietly to his father. Without touching, they walked away together. My heart ached for him.

Izzy, in her peculiar but gentle way, hugged me one more time before disappearing behind the door that read, "Stairs." I can't blame her for wanting to go home.

Joan was already gone. I assumed she was working to continue her mission to save her farm. I reached down and put my heels back on that I had taken off during the ordeal. Tara came storming through the crowd of on lookers and smashed into me with one of her bear hugs. I accepted it with profound gratitude. We strolled arm in arm to my office. We took the stairs. The elevator had plummeted to the fifth floor. Terror filled my mind as I considered how close I came to death and how close he came to me.

I shuffled into my office alone and sat in my overstuffed, high-back armchair. As I glanced around, I realized how bleak it looked in there. Metal windows with dusty blinds filled up one of the walls. My heavy oak desk, shipped from London, sat before me with an empty client chair sitting in front of it. A wilting plant occupied a stand by the door. I chuckled to myself.

"Good to see you kept your sense of humor after such a nightmare today, Sara!" a tremendous voice thundered from the doorway. It was my boss, Mr. Croxley. He was three hundred pounds and his suspenders struggled to hold up his trousers. He reminded me of a penguin character I read about in a comic book when I was a teenager.

Mr. Croxley constantly had chewing gum in his mouth and that drove me insane. "But at least you made it to work!" He continued as he snickered. His belly shook like Santa Claus.

"Mr. Croxley? I hate to tell you this, but…" I couldn't believe what I was doing. "I quit."

I watched the sense of humor leave Mr. Croxley's' sweaty face as the reality of what I said sunk in. His double chin quivered as he struggled to find the right words. I couldn't decide whether he wished to yell at me or beg me to stay. I know I am the best worker he had. It must have stung to watch me leave, but that is just what I did. The further I moved away from my office, down the twelve flights of steps and out to my car, I felt lighter.

After I returned home, I trekked up the stairs to my room. I collapsed onto my bed face down and I cried for the first time in years. After I wept every tear, I sat up and seized my laptop. Years ago, my obsession was writing editorials for the local newspaper. I thought it was time to compose another one. I didn't have time to say what I would do if I lived through the elevator ordeal. It would be for my personal healing. I arranged my fingers on the keys and began.

To the Editor,

Recently, I was involved in a near death experience. I was trapped in an elevator that was on the brink of crashing. The hours that I spent trapped with four strangers seemed like years. I never mentioned it to the others, but I stared death in the face. I don't mean that figuratively. There was a fifth man in the elevator with us. I was the only one to notice him. To suggest he was beautiful would be an understatement. He stood in the elevator the entire time beside me. Mocking me with a condescending smirk, he spoke to me in whispered tones as the others told me their stories. He told me I deserved his presence more than anyone in the elevator. What scared me the most about death was he wore a mirror on his chest. It looked like armor. I saw only my reflection. I didn't like what I saw.

I am ready to tell my story.

I am ready to live.

Zombies of Deadwood

Deadwood... how could I describe such a crappy town? It's not Deadwood, South Dakota. You know the place with all the dead trees? I'm talking about Deadwood, Alabama. You probably never heard of it. After living there my entire life, I wish to God I had never heard of it either. There is nothing to do there. That town puts the "Dead" in Deadwood. You must drive two hours to get to the nearest city, which was something I refused to do. My name is Chris; I'm the last known survivor of the Deadwood tragedy.

I guess I better start from the beginning. I hate to retell this story. If we are going to learn from this mistake, you need to hear what I have to say.

I was a metal head. Yeah, laugh now, but metal music is what I loved more than life it's self. I reviewed music for an online magazine called Metal Doom. I adored my job. They let me work from home. I have a social anxiety disorder and it was a constant struggle. Having a day job, which meant being out in the public, was not in the cards for me. This job fit me like a glove. When my medication was working right, I ventured out into town to check the mail. I received a bunch of packages from Metal Doom. When I was feeling balanced, I would go pick them up. I had no car. I had to walk at least a mile to town.

Deadwood was buzzing with talk of a new factory coming to town. It would create jobs in a struggling economy. I snagged a newspaper so I could read about it when I got home. The less I had to spend around people, the better. We were a farming community. Something like this was a big deal.

A sketch of the new factory to be built was on the front page. The editorial stated it would manufacture plastics for toys. They were going to use a chemical I couldn't pronounce. The chemical would make the toy fire and choke resistant. It would also cause the toys to have a sour taste, like lemons. The taste was to discourage children from placing the toys in their mouth. You would think people would see right through that, but not around here. Deadwood only saw the dollar signs. The town's mayor wrote an article. He explained how he was going to use the millions provided by the factory to wake up our quiet town. He was going to build an outlet mall and maybe open a casino to bring in tourist. Looking back, I wished I had known earlier about this factory. I would have written an extensive article about the dangers it would bring. I would have said... well, to hell with what I would have said. What difference could it make now?

It took three months to build Skyway Toy Plastics; short amount of time, huh? I thought so too. I went to check it out. It was a two-mile trek. I wore my knapsack to carry some bottled water. I never trusted public water. Metal Doom's founder, Jared, shared my unease about water. He hooked me up with Waterfall Springs. It was the finest water I ever put to my lips. The water came straight from a waterfall in North Carolina. I drink nothing else.

After passing the farm of Mr. Johnson, I noticed I had a sunburn on the back of my neck. The sun beat down on me. It was exhausting me of my energy. I had to keep going, however. I had to see the factory everyone was talking about.

I finally made it to Skyway Toy Plastics. It had an enormous metal chain linked fence around the property. Smoke belched from fifteen smokestacks placed on top of the massive structure. I felt nothing but dread as I stared at the factory they had built. After I saw everything I went there to see; I turned around and headed back home. I returned to my ordinary routine after my curiosity was satisfied. It was three months later after my factory visit that I noticed changes in the town's people.

One day, I had to make a dash to the bakery for my mom. She was out of bread. Talk about someone who kicks up a massive fit if she's preparing dinner and there is no bread. I strode into town and headed to Anthony's bakery. It smelled wonderful.

"Well, if it isn't little Christopher!" Anthony said as I stretched a "shut the hell up" smirk on my face. I despised it when he called me Christopher. He made me feel as if I was eight years old again.

"Hi, Anthony, my mom needs a loaf of bread today and that's it." I answered, seeking to rush him along.

Anthony's grin dropped a little. "What have you been up to? I don't see you in here much," he said as he wrapped up a fresh loaf in a neat plastic bag.

"I, uh… work for a magazine. How much?" I replied, wishing he would cut this brief reunion short.

"Oh, three dollars even." He said as he reached behind his ear and scratched. "I swear, this rash popped up a couple of days ago. It just won't go away." When he pulled his hand away, some of his hair was tangled between his fingers. His fingertips had blood on them. "What the…" He added with a perplexed expression.

"Geez, man, maybe you should go to the doctor for that." I said as I flung a five-dollar bill on the counter. "And keep the change." I added as I hurried out of the store. No way was I going to pick up whatever he had.

I walked slower than usual through town. I was feeling pretty good that day, and the weather felt terrific. I stopped and peered through a few windows. I noticed flyers about the new outlet mall coming, and their store would move there soon. I was so preoccupied that I almost ran into Mandy's baby stroller.

"Why can't you just watch where you're going, huh? You think you own the town, don't you? Don't you!" Mandy shouted.

I had known Mandy since high school. I never saw her yell one day in her life. She used to have a full head of beautiful blonde hair and a smoking hot body. Even after she had her baby, she was still hot. Now, her hair was flat and pale. Her blue eyes looked watery, like she had been sobbing. Mandy's clothes looked like she hadn't cleaned them in a month.

"Mandy, are you ok?" I replied as I sought to approach her.

"Who are you? How do you know my name?" Her eyes flitted around. "Watch where you're going next time, Mr."

As she shuffled away, I peeked down into her stroller. There was nobody in there. I was officially wigging out. I had to get home before I had a panic attack in the middle of town. The last thing I needed to do was to embarrass myself. I quickened my steps.

With each person I passed, I became more frightened. William, the butcher, was standing in the window of his shop chewing on a raw steak. Millie, the dry cleaner, stood outside her store crying. Fred, the newspaper editor, was on the street corner yelling and throwing newspapers at people. I didn't wish to see anymore, so I ran. I ran until I came to the Johnson farm. The stink of copper hit my nose as I wandered past the farm. As I passed the chicken coop, I noticed white chicken feathers on the road. Mr. Johnson stood inside of the coop, unmoving. When he heard my footsteps, he twisted around to face me. He rubbed his bloodstained hands down his overalls. I jumped when he spoke to me.

"They just wouldn't shut up; you know how they cackle. Please don't tell the Mrs." He stated as he walked my way. I spun and sprinted as fast as I could. When I reached home, I bolted all the doors and windows. Mom came barreling out of the kitchen.

"Chris! What in the name of all that is good, are you doing?" She said as she wiped her hands on her apron.

"Everybody has lost their freaking minds! The people in town are acting crazy!"

"Now… it can't be that bad. Come and eat supper."

"I'm not kidding, mom! The butcher was eating uncooked meat, and the baker has an awful rash! When he scratched it, his hair fell out! Farmer Johnson just annihilated his chickens. I swear he was going to kill me!" I replied as I closed the curtains.

"Stop this! Come to dinner." She said as she snapped her fingers and sat down at the table. I reluctantly moved into the kitchen. Since my dad disappeared, I couldn't remember a day when dinner looked like that. The roast was raw and bloody. Everything else on the dinner table was burned. I couldn't make out what it had once been.

"Mom, are you ok?" I said anxiously. My heart sped up as she smacked her head with her palm.

"All these years I cooked, and I slaved for what? For you? You are just like your dad! You always want more. I have nothing to give; nothing!" She stood up, rushed to her room, and slammed the door. I could overhear her smashing glass and shifting furniture around. I moved to her door after working up my courage. I snatched my baseball bat for safe measure.

"Mom, are you ok? Please answer me."

The door lurched open, and she had her suitcase packed. She had her pocketbook and keys. "Get out of my way!" Pushing past me, she stormed out the door. She didn't even take her car; she just wandered into the dark. I watched until I couldn't see her anymore. It didn't take long for me to figure out that I was the only sane person left in town.

As the weeks progressed, I went into survivor mode. I traveled at night to pick up supplies when I ran low. I loaded myself down with the weapons I swiped from the neighbors. The town of Deadwood went from a promising development to a wonderland for zombies. They were alive, but it was a different sort of alive. For example, I saw a couple of people step off the Deadwood lover's leap bridge. With catatonic expressions on their faces, they sunk to the bottom without trying to swim. I witnessed a man squatting on a corner in town, yanking his hair out and eating it.

I had to move to an abandoned warehouse about a mile away from town. The stench of Mr. Johnson's farm was directly upwind. It wasn't just the chickens that stank of death. My mom ran into farmer Johnson and well... you can guess the ending. Mrs. Johnson met the same outcome as my mother. A few weeks later, Mr. Johnson disappeared. I didn't look for him. Would you?

It was late one night. I ran into town to the grocery store to determine if I could pick up some supplies. I successfully broke into the Brown Bag grocery store. I was hoping I could locate some canned meat and bottled water. It was at that moment when I picked up the bottle of water a revelation hit me. The strange things happening to the people started after Skyway Toy Plastics moved into town. I had to go there and find out. Leaving the Brown Bag grocery store, I headed straight for the factory. Nothing moved in those days except for me and the zombies. The animals had dropped dead weeks ago. If anything moved around me, it wasn't good.

After I made it to the chain linked fence, I climbed over. The full moon illuminated Skyway Toy Plastics. Smoke spewing from the stacks put out the illusion the factory was full of workers. The front door was wide open and the lights inside flickered. I was petrified, yet it relieved me to see electricity. I had been living in the dark because of the abnormal actions of the town's people.

When satisfied the factory was empty, I went through the front door. I discovered a map on the wall, and it read, "you are here". It pointed to a lobby outside of the main production floor. I opened the door and the noise of the machines working to pump out plastic made me feel deaf. I searched around and located an emergency off switch and pulled it. The noise gradually came to a standstill. The smell of scorched metal filled my lungs. It made me want to vomit.

I discovered an office up a flight of stairs. I prayed it had a phone or a functioning computer I could use to send for help. The only obstacle I could see was I had to scale over a mountain of mangled plastic to reach the stairs. I stumbled and slipped over the plastic. Cutting myself on the sharp edges of the damaged plastic, I made it to the steps. My ankle screamed in protest with each step I took toward the office. Along with the deep lacerations, I had sprained my ankle in the heap of wasted plastic.

I exhaled a sigh of relief as I approached the office. It was devoid of insane people. For safety, I locked the door behind me. I sat down at the boss's desk and opened the laptop. Thankfully, it had never been turned off or it would have taken forever to crack the password. I saw a blinking red file in the corner. I went against my fear of viruses, and I clicked on it. A video screen popped up. The camcorder was pointing at the spot I was sitting in. A man with grey hair and a beard came into view.

"My name is Professor Weston. I am the creator of Skyway Toy Plastics. I am leaving this message for whoever I may leave behind. That's if I didn't wipe out humanity as we know it." The professor wiped his brow and continued. "I made a terrible mistake. I thought the synthetic formula I invented to make plastic was safe. Assuming it was harmless enough, I drained the used water from the machines into the creek nearby. I didn't make sure the creek did not run into the town's water supply. Oh God, what have I done? I'm so sorry, I can't fix this. I can feel myself slipping. Whoever you are, if you are capable, take the disk I left behind on the desk. Download the file, The Toy Maker. It should provide the next scientist the formula I used. Hopefully, it will help reverse the damage I have done. Maybe my maker will see that as my penance. I hope, whoever you are, that you too will forgive me someday."

The screen returned to the home page. I felt strange. I wondered if Skyway Toy Plastics water pollution had extended to the next town or further. My mind crawled with dread. The only people I knew to contact were the FBI. I went to their website, and I left an email. On the subject line, I wrote S.O.S. I told them where I was. I gave them the number of the phone in the office, and I waited. No one called.

The next morning, the sound of a helicopter landing on the rooftop woke me. I seized the disk with the Toy Maker file and the video. I headed to the roof. Two soldiers cautiously approached me with rifles pointing. I raised my hands in submission.

"What's your name?" The soldier yelled.

"I'm Chris! I sent the email!" I answered as the breeze generated by the helicopter whipped my hair around. The two soldiers looked at each other and silently agreed I was ok. They snatched me by my shirt and stuffed me into the helicopter. It took mere seconds, and we were on our way. "And that brings me back to where I started, right here recounting this story for the hundredth time." I repeated as I scowled at Sergeant Murphy.

"I'm sorry, son. I have to be precise on the details."

"Come on, man! What the hell happened to Dead-wood? Why us? Why was I the sole survivor?" Tears burned my eyes.

"I have been working to understand that myself, Christopher. Your mom needs you to let this go so you can return home."

"What the hell are you talking about? She's dead!" I answered as I searched around the bare white room with the tinted black window. "And that's Chris, not Christopher!"

"Chris… don't you recognize where you are?"

"I'm in a little white room on an army base. What are you getting at, Sergeant Murphy? You know what went on. Your soldiers came to get me." I replied as panic created a lump in my throat.

"Chris, I'm Dr. Murphy. I have been your physician for the past three months. You're at the Skyway mental facility. You have been here since you terrorized your hometown. Don't you remember?" He responded with a worried expression.

The blood rushed from my face. I felt faint as the memories came flooding back to me. It was I who reached over the counter and ripped a handful of Anthony's hair out. I broke out the butcher's window. He offered me a chunk of raw meat to put on the wound. I pushed Millie down and made her cry. I kicked Mandy's stroller and made her yell at me. It was me that grabbed Fred's newspapers and hurled them on the pavement. Worst of all, it was me standing over Mr. Johnson's chickens with blood all over my clothes. My mother ran from me when she saw me coming toward her with a bat.

It was all falling into place. The room spun as I stood up and glanced around. Dr. Murphy was wearing a white lab coat, not an army uniform. The soldiers who came for me at the lab had been the Emergency Medical Service. The factory I broke into was the clothing factory down the street from my house.

"That's right, Chris. Let the truth flood your mind. You're safe here at the Skyway mental facility. You're safe now and you're going to be ok." Dr. Murphy declared in his best soothing tone as he approached me.

"No! This isn't real! This isn't real! You're lying to me! You're covering up the massacre! You gave me some kind of drug to make me think I did something insane!" I stepped up to the tinted glass and slammed my fist against the window. "Help me! Help me! Someone… help me!"

"No, Chris, this is real." Dr. Murphy said as he drove a needle into my arm. The room swirled with colors.

Everything went black.

The Author

B. D. West is an American author of fiction, children's stories, poetry, short stories, crime, fantasy, supernatural fiction and science fiction. Originally a native of Tennessee, she fell in love with the mountains of North Carolina. The local folklore and artistic culture of the Blue Ridge Mountains have been an inspiration for the tales she prints on paper. B. D. West's words written on paper, the poems spoken from the heart, and the daring fictional worlds she builds for the readers are a tribute to the passion she has for writing stories. Her debut book, Wynter Of Wolves released in 2020, followed by Wynter Of Wolves, The Seven in 2021. B. D. West is an avid reader and a fan of the writings of Edgar Allan Poe. In her free time, she loves walks in the park, reading, traveling, talking with fans on her social medias and spending time with her family.

authorbdwest.com/bdwest